STRANGE ESCAPES

H . BEDFORD-JONES

STRANGE ESCAPES

H. BEDFORD-JONES

WRITING AS GORDON KEYNE

COVER BY
HERBERT MORTON STOOPS

ILLUSTRATIONS BY
EARL BLOSSOM
L.F. GRANT

STEEGER BOOKS • 2025

TABLE OF CONTENTS

STRANGE ESCAPES

THE HAND INVISIBLE

MOST EXCITING OF ALL ADVENTURES IS THAT OF THE ESCAPING
PRISONER—THE LIFE-OR-DEATH CHANCE TAKEN BY A LONE
FUGITIVE AGAINST TREMENDOUS ODDS. THE ABLE AUTHOR
OF "GUNPOWDER GOLD" HAS THEREFORE CHOSEN FOR HIS
NEXT THESE "STRANGE ESCAPES"—A SERIES OF BRILLIANT
STORIES OF WHICH THE FIRST FOLLOWS HEREWITH.

COTTEREL STARED defiantly at his cell-mate. A flush was in his thin cheeks, a burning light in his eyes.

"They can't keep me here!" he snarled under his breath. "They can't! I'll get away. It may take months, years—but I'll do it. They can't keep me here for life. I'm innocent, I tell you! I didn't do it!"

He had been working up to this point of explosion for days. Normally a young man of definite charm, of winning personality, he had become sullen and glowering. Wise old Manning, who had spent half his life in prisons, knew the symptoms and was worried. He had come to like young Cotterel rarely. He had come to believe that this "lifer" was really not guilty of the crime that had sent him here.

To the old man's notion, this prison was a "pipe." The two were allowed to talk. Manning could have his beloved brushes and sketching materials—an expert forger, he was a creator of exquisite pictures; and in comparison with some places, the regulations here were lax. But as old Manning was well aware, they were not careless.

"I tell you, I'm leaving!" Cotterel went on. "I've got it all figured out. You needn't hand me any bunk about getting transferred to Alcatraz if I fail. I don't intend to fail. It may take me months, but I'm not going to stay here."

Manning said nothing, for the best of reasons: his vocal cords were paralyzed. But his long, slender fingers spoke for him.

"Suppose you get bumped trying it?"

"I'll take that gamble," said Cotterel. Since being incarcerated here, he had had plenty of time to learn the finger-talk employed by Manning. "I've made up my mind."

Manning regarded him anxiously. A wise, shrewd old man was this forger; a man of the keenest intelligence in many ways. He had come to feel a real affection for young Cotterel. Time and again he had acted as a buffer, a windbreak. He had saved Cotterel from many an ill-judged impulsive action.

His fingers began to work nimbly.

"You have a plan? You are sure of every detail?"

"Absolutely," said Cotterel with defiant conviction; and Manning nodded.

"Good. I knew you had a brain. You've provided against everything, even the invisible hand and the unexpected message? Splendid! In that case, you're sure to win. Nobody has ever escaped from this place, but you'll do it. Congratulations!"

Cotterel gazed at him with a slight frown.

"I figured you'd try to argue against it. You really think it can be done?"

"Absolutely," said the swift fingers, "under the given circumstances."

"Hm! What d'you mean by that invisible-hand stuff? Radio?"

Manning's wrinkled, prison-gray features relaxed in amused laughter. They sat on the lower bunk together; the indefinable, repugnant odor of clean but massed humanity drifted in upon them, the murmur of sounds from this cell-house hung in the air about them.

Cotterel waited, sensing that the older man's mind was pregnant with unuttered things. He had grown to hold Manning in a peculiar esteem and respect that was beyond mere friendship; criminal or not, the man had a fund of deep, sure wisdom—all the deeper, perhaps, because he was now behind the bars. He himself—guiltless of crime, yet condemned—owed a heavy debt of friendship to this man, and recognized it.

"No, not radio." Manning's fingers were hesitant. "The invis-

*Kermen crouched,
immobile. The sentinel
was approaching.*

ible hand and the unexpected message—two things that nearly every man forgets. One is a certainty; the other a bare possibility. One is here, waiting for you every day. The other may not come for years. By some miracle of the law of averages, they do show up together—well, perhaps once in a century, as they did with the Sieur de Kermen."

Cotterel looked at him, puzzled.

"Damned if I know what you're driving at. Invisible hand? Have you gone nuts all of a sudden, or have you turned spiritualist?"

Manning uttered a silent chuckle. "Neither.... Here, I'll show you where that chap Kermen lived. Hand out the sketches, will you?"

FROM UNDER the bunk Cotterel produced an album of sketches by the hand of old Manning. The latter produced one—apparently the sketch of a fairy island, a solid mass of masonry rising from the sea with its pinnacle in heaven. Battlements lifted from the water; towers lifted farther, buttresses curved in a breath-taking sweep upward, to culminate in a cluster of spiring walls.

Cotterel stared at it, fascinated.

"Well? What's this place?"

Manning caught up a pencil and wrote a few words, for which his nimble fingers then made the symbols.

"One of the most famous prisons in the world; on an island off the Breton coast, the Alcatraz of a bygone day. In fact, they got the idea of Alcatraz from this place. While in the nominal charge of monks, it had a royal commandant and a garrison of soldiers, received the secret prisoners of the King, and was the most dreaded prison in all France. Architects called it the Marvel; France called it the Ocean Bastille; on the maps it was known, and still is, as Mont St. Michel."

"Oh!" said Cotterel. "I've heard of it. Who was what's-his-name?"

"Kermen? The Sieur de Kermen wrote a witty verse about Madame de Pompadour, and that finished him. He was a young Breton noble. He was hauled out of his home between two days and plumped down in Mont St. Michel."

With his pencil, Manning pointed to a spot halfway up the top cluster of masonry.

"There, in this tower, was a cell. In the cell was a massive cage, eight feet square. In the cage was Kermen—for life. This was in the late fall of 1762. Five months later, Kermen escaped. He was one of the few persons who ever accomplished such a feat."

The eyes of Cotterel lit up suddenly.

"Tell me about it! I might get some pointers, eh?"

"You might," was the silent reply. "There was one difference between this place and Alcatraz of the present day. Mont St. Michel was situated on sands that dried for miles about it at low tide—quicksands, in many spots. The prisoners were warned of this, but were not warned of anything else. They mocked at the warning. First, they knew it was impossible to escape. Second, all the communication between the Mont and the mainland passed over the sands when the tide was out; therefore they knew it would be possible to get away, if they could leave the prison. But even did they reach the savage woods of the Breton coast, they would be run down like wild animals."

"Not an encouraging prospect," observed Cotterel. "Still, there might be worse. If the right man tries it, if he plans each detail perfectly, anything is possible."

"So Kermen thought," was the response of old Manning. "Although he was in solitary, there was no rule against his talking. He fell into the habit of talking every day with his guard, Dupont; and of all things, they discussed escape. Dupont was a soldier, a hard, dry, merciless man. He liked to torment the prisoner. But I must tell you more about the prisoner, about his prison, about the impossibility of any escape—"

Cotterel watched those deft, slender old fingers with fascination. He never tired of watching them. Their skilled weaving of words helped to occupy his brain and kill the timeless hell that surrounded him.

Now they were more fascinating than ever, as they sketched Sieur de Kermen—that ardent, eager, hotly impulsive young Breton whose life had so suddenly ended in this cage. It was a cage of massive wooden bars two inches thick, hewed out of oak long centuries ago, a cage more for punishment than for restraint, a final prison within the very heart of a prison. At one end was the thick stone wall with its tiny window.

Kermen was black-browed, resolute, alert of eye and keen of brain. Plucked from his own château in the heart of the Breton forests, he knew next to nothing of Mont St. Michel, but he learned. The danger-lines of his square chin and mouth were masked by a growth of beard. His knotted shoulder muscles were masked by rags; but beneath his quiet acceptance of destiny lay a raging spirit. Like an eagle with clipped wings, he bided his time.

Twice a day, Dupont appeared, opened his cage door, gave him food; the second time, at dusk, Dupont led him out for a half-hour walk on the platform of the tower, watching him narrowly as he paced up and down the stones. From his window he had a view of the distant coast-line and the sands or water about the islet. Those gleaming sands beckoned him to liberty, three hundred feet below.

"Bah! I'll not be here long," he assured Dupont. "My sister has influence. She'll see to it that I get a pardon. Before Christmas, I'll be out!"

CHRISTMAS CAME and passed. The straw covering the stone floor was rotten and alive with vermin. The walls were scaly from the damp sea air. The huge iron lock of the cage door, although kept well oiled, was a rusty shell from the same cause.

Dupont liked to jeer at him. "Once out of the cage, the cell remains, my friend! Once out of the cell, there's still the tower;

This Alcatraz of a bygone day received the secret prisoners of the King; it was the most dreaded prison in all France.

the walls below have soldiers. If you leave the cage, the cell, the tower, and flutter like an angel from the walls to the shore underneath—there's the sea to pass. Pleasant prospect! And if you wait for the tide to go down, you have the quicksands replacing it. Tell me when you want to try it, and I'll enjoy the spectacle."

Dupont would enjoy it, yes. His hard, cruel features backed up his words. He lost no opportunity to sear and scald the prisoner with his burning tongue. There was no kindness or pity in the man.

Kermen never lost his temper, never showed his hatred. He was a model prisoner. When the prior of the abbey came each week to visit him, he never had any complaints. No letters came to him; he wrote none. When he stretched out on the old bed or cot across one end of his cage, and shivered in the wintry wind under his blankets, he did not break into curses and railings against fate.

It did not occur to anyone that the silent man is the dangerous man….

Christmas gone, he gave up hope of hearing anything from his sister. The jeers of Dupont sank into his soul. He had dared

to mock the favorite of the king, and he would be here until he died. Unless he escaped.

He resolved to escape....

From the platform of the tower, the hopelessness of such an attempt was more apparent. Suppose he stood here, free— what then? Below were watch-rooms and a massive gate, from which ran a curved descent of stone stairs to the lower walls— an immense open stairway thirty feet wide, with landings and rest-benches. Anyone gaining the upper buildings had to come by this approach. There was no other. And even if he descended it, the walls below were guarded by soldiers.

Any other descent had to be by air. These upper walls plunged straight down and down. Built as a fortress, this place had never been captured by an enemy.

Kermen, springing up, rushed at him. The man glanced around; before he could cry out, the oak bar descended with crushing force.

The platform of the tower communicated by a battlemented approach with one flank of the abbey buildings where there was nothing at all underneath—nothing but a tremendous gulf that ended on the sand outside the walls. One evening as he paced up and down, Kermen heard a strange noise he had often heard, and now he saw the cause.

A tremendous creaking and groaning filled the air—a sound sufficient to wake the dead. This squealing shriek came from the abbey buildings on a level with his tower platform, probably two hundred feet away. Here had swung into sight an immense crane and wheel, over which ran a rope. This rope, dropping straight down to the sand at the foot of the Mont, was hauling up a tremendous net filled with boxes and barrels.

Dupont, seeing his interest, came closer to him with a thin laugh.

"That's how you're fed, my friend; that's how everything comes up here from below. An interesting invention, eh? I see the idea appeals to you. Easy to come up that way—easy to go down. Yes?"

"So it would seem," Kermen replied.

Dupont chuckled.

"A prisoner tried it once, ignorant that three men are required to work the winch in the kitchen. He went down like a plummet. There's no way of slowing up the rope, you see. Remember it, my friend, remember it!"

Kermen shivered a little, and turned away.

"Thank you for the warning," he said in a disconsolate voice, and Dupont laughed in cruel delight at his dejection.

But, in his heart, Kermen felt a pulsing thrill that he could scarcely repress. The one problem that had baffled him was suddenly solved. Now he had only to overcome a few trifling details.

DETAILS—EACH ONE exact, carefully figured out, perfectly timed. Each day as he paced the tower platform during his little round of liberty, he eyed those ramparts leading to the kitchens of the abbey and above them. He learned every stone in them, every narrow place, every nook and cranny. He watched where the sentinels paced. He spent long night hours figuring out the time and tide. From his little window, he could tell when there was water around the Mont and when the sands were bare; no more, but this was quite enough for his purpose.

In the cold days and shivering nights of January, he settled down to work. All his hope of any intervention with the king was gone; the utter silence of his sister, of his friends, showed that they were afraid to work on his behalf or write him. Anyone who insulted the king's mistress got short shrift in those days. Kermen was not aware that he had been ordered shut up in strict incommunicado; no letters would have reached him, in any case.

His rotted old bed-frame had yielded precious treasure— part of a rusted iron clamp that had served to hold the frame together. This he sharpened on the stones of the wall, rubbing and rubbing eternally until one edge of it was razor-keen. With it he attacked one of the wooden bars of his cage, not to make an opening for egress, but to obtain the lever and weapon he needed.

IT WAS slow work; the ancient oak was almost as hard as the iron. He had the one inestimable advantage of not being watched. The daily inspection of Dupont was a mere casual look around, the weekly visit of the prior held no danger. Thus, he was entirely free to work as he willed, and with the edge of his iron fragment continually re-whetted on the stone, he made progress. He had nothing else to do—except be sure of each detail.

Here he was positive and left no loophole for chance to defeat him. Over and over, his brain covered each phase of each detail; he even made separate plans in case the weather changed suddenly, if rain came or wet fog from the sea. For any contingency that might arise, even discovery of his work and plans, he was fully prepared.

Even to the quicksands. True, he was only allowed out here on the tower platform after darkness had fallen. He could see nothing of the sands around the island. But twice he was out here at ebb tide, when the sands were bare, and he saw the lights of people going to the mainland or returning. He had only to reach the one entrance to the Mont, and then follow a straight course. He took his bearings of that course by the lights, and knew he could laugh at any quicksands. His mind was at rest there.

Thus he satisfied himself; nothing was neglected or over-looked.

With breadcrumb-paste and dirt, he filled the holes he cut in the cage bar before Dupont came each day; not that it was necessary, perhaps, but he could not afford to take the least chance. The holes deepened until a mere shred of oak held the bar in place. He was ready.

His calculations were exact as to time and tide. The mainland was only a mile and a half distant, but to follow the route marked in his mind, from the entrance of the Mont to the little town of Pontorson, was farther. He must so time his escape from the cage, the cell, the tower, the island itself, that when he set foot on the sands below he would have time to reach the mainland, yet not leave time enough for pursuit to follow him. If he reached shore, and the water cut off any pursuit, he could be in safety before it really started after him. While he knew nothing of local conditions, he was certain, by universal geographical knowledge, that from ebb tide to flood tide would require six hours; and on this accepted fact he based his calculations.

These were marvels of ingenuity. He had, of course, no watch, but he had means of marking the time roughly. In minutes, by his own pulse-beats; in hours, by the voice of the sentinels on the ramparts, and by the bells from the abbey up above. Those monks were Benedictines, vowed to silence. Until they retired to sleep, Kermen knew the hour by the sound of the bells. After that, the sentinels would serve him.

There were further complications—to indicate just one, he knew he must kill or remove a sentinel. It must be done imme-diately after that sentinel had voiced his hourly "All's well!";

*When Kermen leaned over him, he found
that the man had died instantly.*

thus, his action would not be discovered for at least an hour. This
action, however, must fit exactly with all the other details of his
plan, lest it disarrange them. And careful figuring was needful.

He set his escape for the night of January twenty-fifth. At
precisely eight o'clock of this night, he would break out the bar
of his cage—after that, every least detail was figured exactly
and precisely. In the event of fog, which frequently came in
very suddenly and thickly, he must postpone the matter until
the next night.

THE DAY came. Another man might have been excited,
in a fever of impatience, all day long; but not Alaine, Sieur de
Kermen. So great was his mental poise, so confident and assured
was he, that he awaited the evening with patience; he even slept
during the day, in order to be fresh that night.

At seven o'clock, Dupont brought his supper and took him
out on the platform for his daily airing. Darkness had fallen; the
stars were clear and cold. No fog. No snow or rain. No moon.
Everything was perfect, as perfect as he could have wished.

Then, as though to give him a good omen, came a curious
incident proving his own mental accuracy. Dupont's lantern
flickered and went out while they were on the platform. Dupont

came back into the cell, tried to relight the lantern, failed, and set it down. When he locked Kermen into the cage, he departed with his usual stinging taunt, and forgot his lantern.

Kermen called after him, called loudly, and he returned, with an oath.

"You forgot your lantern," said Kermen. "I'll not need it when I leave, to-night, so you may as well take it along."

Dupont snarled at him, in evil humor, caught up the lantern, and the cell door clanged shut again.

Kermen drew a deep breath; the unexpected had happened, and he had been equal to it. Unless he had brought Dupont back now, the guard would have returned later for the lantern, probably disrupting all his plans. He had acted well, he felt.

IN THE darkness, he polished off his simple meal, and restrained himself. Until the moment set, he would not so much as touch that cage bar. As he sat, however, he began to quiver a little; trembling seized upon him, and the agony of suspense was terrible. Yet he endured it. Until the voices of the sentinels floated in, announcing that the moment had come, he did not stir.

Eight o'clock. He needed no light; he knew as though it were daylight just where each object was. He had rehearsed every move and act. He went to the cut bar, tried it, put his weight upon it—and broke it.

In his hand was a two-foot section of oak, hard and heavy as iron, two inches thick. He had selected that particular bar with the greatest care.

He turned and went to the cage door. The enormous iron lock had been bolted to the oak a good two centuries ago or more; tradition said the cage dated from the time of Louis XI. Kermen set the bar in his hand exactly as he had planned, against the side of the lock, and put his weight on it. He had judged aright. There was a crackle of rusted metal, and the entire lock broke clear.

He was out of the cage. The first step was accomplished.

He went to the door of the cell. Here his task would have

been impossible, had not his careful attention to the least detail made it absurdly easy. He had a fulcrum for his lever, but here his lever must have a point in order to be of any use. So he had cut one end of the bar on a slant. He inserted this flat point with the greatest care in the spot previously selected by daylight. The lock, which was probably two centuries older than that on the cage, crumpled with a mere wheeze of ancient metal. Another twist, and it came away *in toto*, dragging the bolt with it. There was no bar outside the door.

The second step was accomplished.

Kermen tried the door, found that it opened freely—and left it closed. His iron will conquered the impulse that tore at him in every nerve. Despite the chill of the winter night, sweat streamed down his cheeks as he deliberately went back into the cage and sat down on his bed; his knees were shaking, his fingers were uncertain.

He forced himself to wait here, gradually regaining his composure. At this moment, he knew the sands around the island were dry. Possibly belated visitors were coming or going. If he could gain those sands now, he would not have the slightest difficulty in following them to the mainland. Yet, if he were to reach the sands, he must stick to his plan. And this called for taking care of one sentinel at nine o'clock, not before. He must not risk the least detail.

He waited, grimly. He had given himself this extra time in case of trouble in breaking the locks; no use taking any chances. He attempted to count the passage of time, but failed. This alarmed him. With a stern effort, he got himself in hand, quieted his brain, and settled into a cold concentration. Again luck favored him. A bell sounded; it was the abbey bell denoting that the hospice, or quarters of guests and pilgrims, was closed for the night. He had forgotten all about this bell, which very seldom reached his ears. Eight-thirty, then.

HE COULD begin to count the minutes now, and did so. At ten to nine, he took his bar of oak, left the cage, and went out on the platform. He turned to the ramparts, those which led above the kitchen of the abbey.

A sentinel was there, pacing up and down in the starlight; now close at hand, then to the far end of the section. Kermen crouched, immobile. Once more luck was with him. The sentinel was approaching when the first of the hourly calls floated up from other sentries on the lower ramparts.

The man came close to where Kermen waited, turned, and then uttered his own call to show that he was awake. It was taken up in turn by another, and passed on; but this sentry came to a sudden halt. Kermen, springing up, rushed at him. The man glanced around; before he could cry out, the oak bar descended with crushing force.

When Kermen leaned over him, he found that the man had died instantly.

From the dead man, he took firebox, knife, and the crossed belts of his uniform, with the belt proper. These, with his own belt, gave him four; he buckled them together and then moved on along the parapet, taking musket and bayonet.

He paused. Directly below him was the huge crane and wheel by which provisions and luggage were brought to the abbey from far below. Around one of the projections of the battlement, he passed the four belts and made them fast. Holding to this encircling strip of leather, he let himself out and down until his feet came to rest on the crane.

Ten feet below was the huge window-opening into which the net of goods was swung; it was far beyond his reach, as he had figured it must be. With the fixed bayonet of the musket, however, he could reach the rope that passed through the wheel and went into this window below.

He clung to the belt by one hand, and reached out. He stood above a sheer gulf, straining far by one hand; if that string of belts gave way, he was gone on one plunge. Even though the night was windless, air circled around him and tore dangerously at him. Twice the bayonet found the rope, only to let it slip. His arms were growing weary, the frightful strain of his position was overcoming him, when the bayonet caught the rope and drew it.

For an instant his heart leaped, as the wheel creaked; then the rope came up to him, drawn not from the wheel, but from the window. Desperately, he inched his hand along the musket, balancing its weight, until he got his fingers on the rope. Then he drew himself back to the parapet. Giddy, trembling in every muscle, he fell across the stone and let the rifle down inside.

For five minutes he lay there, weak and a little sick, but holding to the rope. Recovering, he pulled himself over and began to drag in on the line. It came up to him from the coils inside the window, below—a stout, thick rope, but flexible with age and long use.

HE PULLED it in—in—until he had as much as he could carry—more than enough to serve his purpose. Then, with the soldier's knife, he sawed through it, shouldered the coil, and went back to the parapet of his own tower. He had now to manage the third step; his escape from this tower.

About one of the projections of the battlement,—a very particular one,—he passed the rope, and then lowered it. Directly below was the ascent going up to the impregnable entrance of the abbey proper, one of whose guardian towers was this on which he stood. No guards were posted on the huge, curving sweep of masonry, the giant staircase leading down from the abbey to the lower walls; but sentinels were dotted along those walls below, which rose up straight from the rocks of the sea. So Kermen had to exercise caution.

He let down the rope, and from the sense of feel, could tell that it reached the stones below and hung there. Not enough. Leaving it in place, he returned to where he had obtained it. Against just such need, he had weighted the end of the cut line with the soldier's musket. Now he hauled up more rope and more, from the tremendous lengths coiled in the kitchen opening below. Again having enough, he cut it, shouldered the coil, and went back to his tower platform.

No alarm below; his dangling rope had attracted no attention. Now he lowered the second length, came to the end, let it go altogether, slipping and slithering down through the air and over the starlit masonry below.

N O M O R E time to kill now—on the contrary, everything depended on fast work. Kermen let himself over the dizzy edge, swung down on the rope, caught it with his feet, and descended. Easily said; but a mad thing for a man innocent of ropes to attempt. He banged against the tower, burned his hands on the rope, and the enormous strength of his arms and shoulders hardly compensated for his lack of skill. He went down the final ten feet with a rush, but lay quiet when he struck the huge stairs. No alarm was given. No bones were broken. He came to his feet, caught up the rope that lay loosely on the descent, and peered ahead.

One more step was accomplished. Now to leave the island itself.

He knew exactly where he wanted to use the second rope. In the starlight, the figure of the nearest sentry was visible; out beyond, the sands lay bare. His rope coiled, Kermen crept down along the wall of the towers until he reached the outer line of battlements. He gained them, saw the sentry a little beyond, watched him pace up and down. When the man's back was turned, Kermen crept out and swiftly made fast the rope about a parapet, sent the coil slithering over, came back to cover.

When the sentry faced about again, he himself followed, regardless of bleeding hands. He was through the embrasure and out of sight, before the sentry turned. Here was his last risk, his final gamble with destiny, as he thought. If that sentry heard him, he was lost. If not, then he won.

When he scraped and swung against the lower wall, he desperately clung to the naked stones, lest he be heard. As he slipped on down the rope, his heart turned over at a sudden sharp voice above—then came a laugh, and he relaxed. Two sentries had met and were standing talking together. Kermen's nostrils caught a faint reek of tobacco smoke. At the same instant, his feet touched something solid.

He was on the rocks below the walls. His escape was accomplished.

Now for safety! Mindful of the two guards talking above, he seized the chance to leave the walls themselves unobserved. The starlight would not betray him to these careless sentries, except at close quarters.

Without hesitation, he struck straight out from the Mont; he had to risk the quicksands here, but found none.... Straight out, fearing at each instant that his figure might be noticed in the light of the high stars; but it was not. No alarm sounded.

He circled around swiftly and struck into the line whose bearings he had noted, heading for the village of Pontorson on the far shore. The sands stretched dry, outspread, level for miles and miles.

And then, all of a sudden, the invisible hand clutched down. Kermen, looking at the sands ahead of him, saw a river appear where, an instant before, had been nothing. Across the night, he heard the rushing ripple of water.

The invisible hand! The one thing against which all cleverness was useless. The one unknown quantity which always obtains, when matched with men's wits.

OLD MANNING leaned back; his deftly flying fingers fell in his lap; their speech was, for the moment, at an end. Cotterel, who had been following the story with absorbed intentness, spoke out impatiently.

"But I don't understand! You say he had escaped—he was correct in everything he planned! And you spoke of a message."

Manning nodded.

"Yes," said his fingers, clicking out the words. "Yes. With the next low tide, a courier arrived. A pardon had been obtained by his sister; he was to be set free. But he was already free, poor fellow!"

"What the devil are you driving at?" demanded Cotterel impatiently.

"T H E   I N V I S I B L E   hand had freed him—the one thing which always puts the cleverest brain to naught," came the response. "There is always something unforeseen, something unguessed, something unknown. In this case, you will remember that Kermen had based all his calculations on the fact that it's six hours from the ebb tide to the flood tide."

"Of course. Any fool knows that," Cotterel interjected.

Manning regarded him for a moment, and smiled a little.

"Of course. But Mont St. Michel happens to be one of the few places in the world where the tide may rise in an hour, in twenty minutes, in five minutes! Sometimes it comes in across the miles of level sands, suddenly fills the channels of unseen rivers, springs out of the sand itself, comes rushing and flooding at a speed nothing can escape! This was one of those times."

"You mean—good Lord! Then this fellow was caught by the tide?"

"Precisely. As every man who matches his wit with the invisible is caught—by something. The man who is so sure he cannot fail, the man who guards against every contingency, the man who refuses to accept what fate has brought to him—that man is the victim of the invisible hand, of the unexpected message. In Kermen's case, the two came together. They rarely coincide, like that, but they did in this instance."

Cotterel stared at him for a moment with slowly whitening face.

"I see," he said in a low voice. "I see what you're driving at. You're telling me there's always hope, that I may be pardoned when I least expect it?"

"That's always the possibility; but what I'm telling you is to warn you against what you can't see, my friend."

"Yeah; I get that too," Cotterel rejoined, and his head drooped. "There's always something—the invisible hand! Well—I'll think about it, Manning. Maybe you're right, at that."

And he stared thoughtfully, soberly, reflectively, at the floor of the cell.

THREE ELECTRIC WORDS

THREE WORDS STRONG ENOUGH TO HOLD A DESPERATE MAN FROM SUICIDE, PERHAPS THE MOST IMPORTANT PHRASE IN OUR LANGUAGE, FORM THE BASIS OF THIS SECOND OF MR. KEYNE'S SERIES OF "STRANGE ESCAPES"—THE ESCAPE OF PORFIRIO DIAZ FROM PRISON.

COTTEREL WAS in one of his horrible moods of black despair.... Young, impulsive, ardent, he was the exact opposite of his cell-mate. He had much to learn, and long to learn it; he was a lifer now.

In all this place of doomed souls, Cotterel was the one person whose plea of "Not guilty" had been entirely true. For him, the outside world was gone forever; this fact of innocence made the horror of it all the worse. At times, the agony became insupportable, and he writhed in a torment past endurance. He had won the liking, the profound pity, the real friendship, of the older man.

Now, lifting tortured eyes, he addressed Manning.

"D'you know I've been in this hell for seven months?" he said hoarsely. A deep breath, almost a groan, escaped him. "Seven months! It's been like seven years. And it's all hopeless, hopeless! I did think of escape. No use. I don't want to escape now. What's the use?" His words pointed the unuttered thought of his brain. Manning, from his experience, knew precisely what terrible thought lay there.

Manning regarded him with compassion, then picked up one of the brushes before him and dipped it. The movement, the action, caught Cotterel's attention.

The gray features of the older man were tired with ills and years, but his sunken old eyes were bright. He was intelligence

personified. Manning knew everything, except what he had most needed to know. He was not in this prison unjustly.

He did not speak. He could not. He was dumb. A forger, yet an artist of supreme talent, during these long months he had taught Cotterel the language of the fingers. It was not such a bad place, this prison. They had many liberties. Manning could make his sketches and drawings; they could talk if they so desired; yet it was prison.

Leaning forward, Manning used his brush to write two words. With a pen, he would have written them exactly as the owner of the name would have signed it. Even with the brush, so delicate was his skill that any official of a past generation acquainted with the signature, would have pronounced it genuine. It was the signature of Porfirio Diaz.

He contemplated it for a moment, then passed it to the younger man.

Cotterel stared at it, and lifted puzzled eyes to the older man. "The old dictator of Mexico? What do you mean by that?"

Manning hesitated slightly. If Cotterel wanted to be free of this prison, it would be easy enough; the guards would shoot to kill. Cotterel was at the point where suicide beckoned him. Manning knew the symptoms.

"Escape hopeless," said Manning on his fingers. "Life hopeless."

"That's it," Cotterel said harshly. "Even if I escape, what good? My life would be empty, shadowed, a living terror. I've nothing to live for."

"No," said Manning's hand. "As long as you think only of yourself, that's true. Look, now. Here's a man. I knew him well."

Swiftly his brush dipped again, and he began a quick sketch. He had the interest of Cotterel, which was what he most desired. He too knew the awful beat of that suicide impulse. He knew how it hammered at the brain until—clang! The decision was formed, the act was taken. He must prevent Cotterel from reaching that point.

The sketch grew under his hand. The figure of a man in a prison cell, looking from a barred window. Below were roofs; the man was in a high cell, somewhere. Just a mere suggestion of a picture. The face of the man was the one striking thing; vigorous, hardy, balanced in its strength and resolution; iron features, giving the lie to vacillation and despair. Eyes with drooping heavy lids of shrewdness.

WITH A gesture, Manning passed the sketch to Cotterel, who studied it frowningly.

"Diaz? You knew him?"

Manning nodded: "Porfirio Diaz." His nimble fingers began to fly. "He too had been just seven months in prison; a real prison, not a summer resort like this. Diaz, at thirty-five a general of division, the one leader on whom all Mexican patriots depended—now defeated, broken, captured, ruined, lost; at any moment, perhaps, facing a firing-squad—kept seven months like a caged bird. The French and Austrians were supreme over all Mexico. Their emperor, Maximilian, held the country in his grip. The scattered forces of the patriots had been smashed. No wonder the thought of suicide came over the mind of Diaz in flooding waves. Do you know what happened? What the background of this situation was?"

Cotterel shook his head, gloomily. Diaz be damned! His own plight was what absorbed him right now. Yet—

"What did happen?" he asked, with a spark of curiosity.

"Nothing happened until Diaz stopped thinking about himself, depending on himself, grieving for his own fate. It's only when a man is so beaten to his knees that he realizes himself utterly futile, that forces are started in motion, somehow. You may call it psychology or you may call it God. Sometimes the man goes on to suicide, and sometimes he rises above that point."

A queer statement to come from a convict! It jerked at Cotterel and caught his attention.

His eyes fastened upon the slim, deft fingers of Manning. A certain concentration was necessary to translate the movements of those fingers into words; and these words, again, into the scenes and action and thought they described.

Here was a cruel, grim and bloody story, said the fingers, and an amazing one in its results. Look at the sketch again. Get the feel of the man gazing out through the bars of his Puebla prison, high in Fort Guadeloupe with the city outspread below. The man who had risen so high, who had fallen so far! Before the barred grating of his cell door was a soldier in Austrian uniform, to typify the foreign grip that had fastened upon Mexico.

No wonder suicide beat with insidious reiteration at the brain of Diaz as he stood there, lost in the contemplation of his own hopeless misery.

His evening meal arrived. A dumpy brown woman came trudging with the tray; a native woman, half Indian, singing to herself a monotonous lilt of dreary song as she came, her flat face vacuous and empty. To the Austrian guard she was a picturesque and ugly creature; to his ears, her mumbling song meant nothing at all. But Diaz, hearing the words, fully conversant with the patois to which he had been born, clenched his hands suddenly and turned. The words hit him like a blow.

"The eagle must fly, the eagle must fly! He must hold the snake in his claws. He must look in the bottom tortilla. Soon he will fly, if he looks in the bottom tortilla. Look carefully. Tomorrow evening be ready. I will come again with word."

The Austrian unlocked the cell door. The brown woman trudged in. She shot Diaz one lightning glance, caught his gaze, and looked at him no more. She knew the words had been understood. She set down the tray, took that from his noon meal, and trudged away again, with her mumbling song. This time, the words meant nothing at all.

Diaz sat down. He had a cot, a chair, a small table—nothing else. On the tray was a meal by no means sumptuous: a plate of tortillas or baked corn-cakes, a pitcher of coffee, and a bowl of chili con carne. It was the usual fare.

DUSK WAS falling, gathering about the hill city of Puebla, bluing the roofs. Bugles shrilled in and about the fortress. Another Austrian appeared; he came into the cell while the guard watched, saluted Diaz, and lighted the table lamp. Already, he observed, Diaz was attacking his meal avidly.

The two Austrians stood outside, talking and laughing together; for the moment he was free of observation. Deftly he slid out the tortilla that was on the bottom of the pile, cut it open with the wooden knife allowed him, saw a slip of paper.

This he quickly removed; transferred it to a pocket. Then he went on with his meal. The sentry at the door was idly watching him again.

His heart pounded. So he was not forgotten! That Indian woman was in the kitchens of the fort, was employed here, was returning tomorrow night. Be ready then—why? No matter. Emotion shook him, but his stolid mien gave no hint of it. The reaction from his mood of utter despair—a mood of only a few moments before—was terrific.

He dared not try to read the message just yet. While treated with respect, he was watched with rigorous care; he was the outstanding patriot general, the one man who was able to meet the French in the field on equal terms. Not even Marshal Bazaine had managed to beat Diaz, but rank treachery. They had offered him parole, and he had refused it; hence they watched him the more carefully.

IT WAS a war of blood, of slaughter, of extermination in some provinces. The United States, engaged in its own life-or-death struggle, protested against a European yoke being fastened on Mexico, but could not intervene. There was talk of an entire province,—all Sonora—with its mineral wealth, being ceded to France. Mexican blood in general accepted the Austrian rule, but Indian blood fought savagely for freedom. Diaz had just enough Indian blood to give him fierce independence of spirit.

All that night he lay helpless to read the message, his blood pounding, his brain in turmoil. Then, when morning came, when sunrise gave him the chance to read it surreptitiously, his pulses leaped again. Nothing about himself there, nothing about his own plight, except by inference; just a few lines of tiny writing, enough to show that some intelligence was at work:

"I shall give that promise when the last foreigner has left the soil of Mexico."

> *The Confederate States have surrendered. Juarez is obtaining a loan of thirty millions in New York. We need you.*

Thirty millions! The war in the north at an end—money and men coming to help freedom in the south! Juarez, president of the phantom Mexican republic, still fighting!

The surge of exultation, of astounded hope, that filled the soul of Diaz was beyond description. In a moment, everything had changed. No longer was it a question of himself, of his own petty fate; during these months of enforced solitude, things had happened in the world. Now destiny was beckoning.

All this and more was summed up in the three electric words: *We need you!*

Somehow the hot day dragged past. As he read the few old books allowed him, as he paced up and down in the blistering courtyard of the fortress at his exercise, as he counted the long hours, Diaz thought of only one thing. Escape! Not for himself now. He had been futile, helpless to aid himself, dragged down by his own existence. Now his horizon broadened. His own puny destiny mattered no whit; but others needed him. The thought wakened everything latent in him, broke out unsuspected energy, spurred his brain into sudden life. He was, literally, a new man.

The Austrians and French drilling down below; the Mexican levies, the guards, the cannon—and against these, the words of a brown woman. The eagle with the snake in his claws; old Aztec symbol of this very land, this people. The eagle must fly; but how?

His cell was in a corner of the upper building that rose in a tower. His window afforded no hope, even could he remove the bars, for the wall below fell away sheer to the ground. His inner door of wood, open during the day for coolth, was closed at night and barred; the outer iron grating was also closed and locked.

Diaz himself could dispose of all these obstacles. His nostrils quivered as he considered them, and thought of the eagle with the snake in his claws. Beyond the door lay the corridor and the stairs that went down to the courtyard. Soldiers here, practically at all hours; the officers' quarters were here, the barracks of the French lay just beyond. Those of the Austrians and Mexican troops were on farther, barring any approach to the fortress gates; those gates, too, were closed with darkness.

A S H E paced the courtyard that afternoon, Diaz saw a group of Mexican soldiers pass. They looked at him and laughed, and paused to gibe at him. One of them, a strapping young fellow, approached him with a jeer.

"So this is the great Diaz, eh? Good afternoon, señor! Our hacienda and all it contains is yours, even to the knives at our belts!"

The Austrian guards promptly assembled and drove off the Mexican soldiers. Diaz was used to insults from his own people who were of the imperial party; he shrugged and went on. Nothing mattered now. He was counting the hours, the very minutes. What would happen? How could he escape? He had not the least idea....

When his exercise-time was up, an officer and a file of guards took him in charge. Instead of returning to his cell, he was led before the commanding officer. It was all very polite, quite merciless and efficient. Orders concerning him had arrived. His word not to serve against the imperialists, and he was free. Otherwise, more rigorous confinement and a move.

"A convoy is departing tomorrow for Mexico City," said the officer. "Unless you wish to be taken with it, give me your parole."

Diaz gave no hint of his inner torture. It was intolerable that this should happen now, at the very instant when hope beckoned him! More rigorous confinement, perhaps a new trial, a firing-squad. He looked impassively at the officer.

"I shall very gladly give that promise," he said, "when the last foreigner has left the soil of Mexico."

The other shrugged and ordered him taken to his cell.

Once there, he stripped off his sweat-wet uniform coat and waited, impassive and outwardly with no emotion whatever. Inwardly, he was on fire. It was tonight or never. If they took him to Mexico City and plunged him into some of those old Spanish dungeons, he could abandon all hope.

His unknown friends who were working here to free him, could not know of these changes, of this threat. Could he reach them, get word through that old Indian woman? Uncertainty and suspense tore at him. Then, as he lay, he suddenly quivered. He could hear her trudging step outside, her monotonous voice singing a native song. Tensed, he listened and caught the words.

"You saw my son. It was he who taunted you in the patio. He will come when the first guard is changed. Be ready."

Diaz sank back in relief. This night or never, then!

THE WOMAN came in, gave him a glance, then ignored him. She retired, and the guard locked the iron grating anew.

*He came back dragging something heavy.... "Here,
señor. You must put on this uniform and cap."*

When the first guard was changed? That would be eight
o'clock, when his inner door was locked for the night. So that
man had deliberately drawn his attention in the courtyard?
Clever fellow. Would he be one of the guards? No; only Austrians were posted here, or French. Another hour to wait.

The prisoner ate and drank by the light of his lamp. He
composed himself, forced himself to betray no signs of excitement. He thought back to the previous day, to his temptation to
suicide, with incredulous horror; what a difference now! What
a difference in himself, in his whole attitude of mind! Win or
lose, this night would end it all; and he would win, he must win.
Not for himself, but for those who needed him. This was war.
And when it came to war, Porfirio Diaz could be as relentless
as any Frenchman.

The guard was changed. His doors were closed and locked for
the night, his lamp was removed, he was alone in the darkness.
From his window, he looked out and could see no stars. The sky
had hazed over. Good!

He waited, more tensely than ever, and at last he heard a sound. The key was being turned in the iron grating. After a moment, the bars of the inner door were very quietly removed. The door opened to show an oblong of very dim light—outside, lanterns hung at the corners of the corridor or gallery, which overlooked the courtyard.

Against this oblong of light, showed the dim, vague figure of a man.

"Señor?" came a low voice. Diaz replied softly.

"I am here. Who are you?"

"Simon Montemayor, señor. I was sergeant in your Nuevo Leon regiment. You do not remember me. Wait!"

The shape of the man disappeared. Presently he came back, dragging something heavy, something he set down inside the doorway. He fell to work over this object.

"Here, señor," came the voice again. "You must put on this uniform and cap."

Diaz was not the man to shrink from wearing those garments. He took them, stripped in the darkness, and put them on. As he took the cap, Montemayor rose, caught at the wall, and stifled a grunt.

"What's the matter?" demanded Diaz.

"I was clumsy, señor. His bayonet got me in the hip."

"Come here."

Montemayor obeyed. All in the darkness, Diaz examined the wound, found it to be a nasty gash, and managed to bandage it with the shirt of the dead Austrian.

And as he worked, Montemayor talked with him in low-breathed words.

Alone? Yes, except for his mother. There was only one possible chance; this was to stroll forth openly, like two soldiers of the garrison. To leave by the gates was out of the question. It must be by the ramparts. Montemayor had ropes hidden there, but they might run into danger. Seeking the cool night air, many of the men sometimes roamed the ramparts or even slept there. This must be risked.

"Ready, then," said Diaz, his tunic buttoned, his belt in place. For weapon, he had the Austrian's bayonet; safest to leave the man's rifle here. "Will your mother be in danger tomorrow, when this is discovered?"

MONTEMAYOR LAUGHED. "She's not known to be my mother, señor. Even if she were, it would not matter. What we do, is for liberty."

Diaz repressed a grunt. Not for him, but for liberty; nothing personal in all this business. For months, this man had been preparing against such a moment, enlisting in the imperialist regiment stationed here, biding his time, making his plans. Now the moment had come—not for Diaz, but for liberty.

"Did you write that news your mother delivered?"

"Yes, señor. I can read and write."

"Good. If we get out of here alive, you shall be Colonel Montemayor. Let's go."

They were off on the instant, walking openly down the corridor toward the stairs, passing the lantern there and coming face to face with the next sentry. Montemayor made some remark in halting German, and the sentry laughed. Then Diaz was past the lantern and on the stairs.

WHEN THEY turned into the courtyard, he noticed that his guide was limping slightly. He could not marvel sufficiently at this man, who had been sent by nobody to do this work. The fellow had written that message, too; a clever thing. Strange, how such a man could take upon himself such a task, for the sake of liberty!

The courtyard, at this hour, held passing officers, groups of men, French or Austrian. Hence it was far safer for the two than it would have been later, when the sentries would be more inclined to notice everyone who passed. Diaz led the way, with the other at his elbow. No one paid them the least attention.

It was when they had passed on toward the gates of the fort, that the first bad break came. A Mexican officer, puffing at his *cigarillo*, was sauntering along when his eye fell on Montemayor. He turned toward them with a bark.

"You, Montemayor! What are you doing here? I refused to give you leave tonight."

At this, Diaz comprehended what risks the man had taken. He stepped forward and saluted the officer, and spoke in his own fluent Spanish.

"Señor Capitan, orders from headquarters. I was directed to find one of your men who could speak some German. The responsibility is mine."

The Mexican officer grunted with astonishment at hearing such fluent speech from an Austrian, but waved his *cigarillo* and passed on, appeased.

"The captain of my company," Montemayor breathed; and Diaz laughed.

"So I gathered. Lead the way to the ramparts. Must we go far?"

"Unfortunately, yes. To the side away from Loreto."

They went on. The two forts of Guadeloupe and Loreto were close together; quite obviously, the walls must be scaled at the safest possible point. When they reached the steps that mounted to the ramparts, Montemayor came to an abrupt halt.

"Señor, it is difficult to walk. I can tell you where the ropes are hidden. The road is only a few hundred yards away. Men with mules are waiting there; they can be trusted. If you go on—"

"Be quiet," ordered Diaz curtly. "We go together. Here, give me your arm."

They gained the ramparts above. Groups of men were in sight, but none were close at hand. Montemayor rested for a moment, and renewed his plea that Diaz go on without him.

"You are the one who matters," he said simply. "For you, Mexico waits; not for me. I have only one ambition, which I shall never attain. It is different with you, señor. If anything happens to you, our country is lost."

"Save your breath," Diaz rejoined. Montemayor shrugged, then uttered a laugh.

"Let's hope I don't need it to whistle with," he said, but gave no explanation of his words.

They went on. Occasional sentries, occasional groups of men smoking and talking; here in the fortress, discipline was not too strict.

THEY CAME to a bastion built out over the sharp hillside, and here, with a low word, Montemayor halted and leaned against the parapet in sharp dejection. No need of talk. Diaz understood instantly, upon learning that the rope was hidden beneath the second cannon whose dim shape rose before them.

Beside that cannon lounged two men, their pipes alight, their guttural German showing them to be Austrians. But, in the corner not twenty feet away, a group of vociferous French soldiers had placed a lantern and were gathered about it playing cards under shelter of the parapet. To get at the rope, the two Austrians must be removed. This might be done at a pinch—but not with those French so close at hand.

"The devil!" muttered Diaz. "We shall have to wait."

"Impossible, señor," said the other at his ear. "Your escape may be discovered at any moment. If we wait, we're lost. Well, no one ever made a broom without making a handle! Now we shall have to get my mother to help. She promised to be waiting down there if we needed her."

He sent a low, musical whistle down at the darkness.

The Frenchmen heard it and looked up from their game. The two Austrians turned. For a moment nothing at all happened. Montemayor broke into a few words of his very unfluent German, which appeased the curiosity of those beyond. And then, with startling abruptness, a shrill voice lifted from down below. It was such a voice as only a Mexican woman torn by passionate emotion can upraise—a wild, furious gabble of words.

From Montemayor came an excited exclamation, half in laughter.

"The French are quartered there—trust her to pick the right place!"

LOUDER, MORE shrill and high, lifted that voice in accusation and alarm. Diaz, perfectly comprehending the torrent of speech, remembering what that brown woman looked like, could not repress a chuckle of amusement. For she was complaining of assault and outrage, complaining to high heaven!

A French voice chimed in with no less frantic protest; the voices of other Frenchmen arose. Obviously, she had accused some passing soldier of insulting her, and now there was the very devil to pay.

"Ha! Listen to that, comrades!"

One of the soldiers by the lantern leaped up. From below, the frenzied babble of voices became wilder, all dominated by the steady flow of emotional speech from the woman. That torrent of words never ceased. It lifted above every other sound. As the voices of Frenchmen tried to drown it out and failed, the group of soldiers around the lantern abandoned their game. With bursts of laughter they went scurrying away to join in the fun and the scandal.

"Quick, señor—before they return we must be gone!" said Montemayor. "My knife—your bayonet!"

The two Austrians had not budged. Probably they did not understand either French or Spanish; they still lolled over the gun, puffing at their pipes. There was only one thing for it; the job must be done while that shrill squabble was still rising to drown out any sound of conflict here.

Diaz had his bayonet bared, as Montemayor limped forward.

It was over quickly; a scuffle of feet, a cry, a broken pipe on the stones. A swift and grim business, grimly done, swiftly finished. Then the coils of rope were snaked out from beneath the gun-carriage. The end was made fast, the coils were flung over the parapet. Already the noise below was quieting.

Montemayor wiped his knife, tucked it away, and hauled himself over the edge of the parapet.

Diaz stood waiting.

As he waited, he looked back to where things were quieting down now. The utter strangeness of it all struck upon his mind; his own destiny, the fate of Mexico, perhaps the star of an emperor—all hinging upon the voluble outcry of a woman accusing a soldier of insult! It was one of those queerly fantastic things which happen in actual life—

A shake of the rope came to his hands, and wakened him. He edged himself over the stones, gripped the rope desperately, and was on his way. There was no great distance to go; a scant forty feet. Yet it seemed a long time until he heard the encouraging voice of Montemayor. Then the ground, sharply falling away into the darkness, strewn with brush and cactus.

They did not need to make swift progress now; they could not, for the blackness was intense. Presently Montemayor ventured a low whistle; it was answered from somewhere beyond, and the two men relaxed. The mules were waiting. There was no alarm from the fort above. They were safe.

"Tell me," said Diaz as they rested a moment. "You spoke of an ambition, my friend. What is that ambition which you can never hope to fulfil?"

The other uttered a soft laugh.

"A dream, señor; the dream of more than one man who stakes his life for this country of ours, for liberty. The dream that some day it may be my hand which leads that accursed Austrian, Maximilian, to the wall, and puts a bullet through him!"

PORFIRIO DIAZ' strong hand tightened on the arm of the man who had saved him.

"Very well, Colonel Montemayor," he said, and his voice echoed the savage softness that had come from the other man's lips. "Very well. I promise it. Your ambition shall one day come to pass. There are the mules—come!"

They melted into the darkness and were gone. And it was

less than two years later, on a June day in 1867, when Emperor Maximilian faced the firing-squad commanded by Simon Montemayor. Diaz never forgot a promise....

The flying fingers of the old forger ceased to move, and fell listless. His bright eyes were on the face of Cotterel, who sat still spellbound by the story he had just watched on those fingers. He looked up at Manning and drew a deep breath.

"I get what you're driving at," he said slowly, reflectively. "We're pretty good friends, Manning. You're trying to drum into me the idea that I've got to quit feeling sorry for myself, play a man's game, and all that. Well, you're wrong! There isn't a living soul on the outside, to give a damn about me—you know what that means? Can you realize it? I've no family. I'm alone."

Manning's hand jerked up. "So am I," his fingers replied.

"Then you can realize all of it." Cotterel shook his head. "No. Rise above any thought of suicide, you say? Easily said, Manning. This man Diaz had a country, a cause. I haven't. He had some one to say those three electric words, as you called them: We need you! Well, I haven't. That's what makes this place an intolerable hell."

Manning leaned forward and looked at him intently. The deft fingers rose. They hesitated for an instant, then they began to signal earnest words, as earnest as the intent look in Manning's face.

"Perhaps you're wrong about that, my friend. Perhaps you, like Diaz, think that because this voice has never come to you, there is no voice."

The younger man laughed again, harshly, bitterly.

"I ought to know! If there was anyone in the world—well, it'd make a difference, of course. But there's not."

"There is," said the fingers of Manning. Frowning, Cotterel looked into those bright, intent eyes.

"What? How the devil do you know so much?"

"Perhaps," said Manning,—and so earnest was his look that

he almost seemed to be speaking the words,—"perhaps I should know better than anyone else. I'm the one who needs you."

Cotterel caught his breath; and then stared into Manning's face, his eyes suddenly widening with comprehension.

THE BREAK'S TONIGHT

A HUNCH—"THE HEART HAS ITS REASONS, WHICH REASON ITSELF CANNOT UNDERSTAND"—IS A VITAL FACTOR IN THIS FASCINATING THIRD STORY OF THE "STRANGE ESCAPES" SERIES.

MANNING WAS worried, deeply worried. The old forger, who was now behind these bars for the rest of his natural days, watched his cell-mate with a knowing eye. Something was wrong with Cotterel. Something was brewing and stewing in the younger man. Within this past week, Cotterel had lost his ardent, impulsive spirit; he was brooding.

Not that he lacked cause. Cotterel was a lifer too, cut off from the world just when life was sweetest and at its bloom. Unlike the older man, Cotterel was not guilty; of this, Manning had convinced himself. The murder charge had been pinned on him by circumstantial evidence. Cotterel took it on the chin, took it like a man; but the long weeks and months must have their toll, and now something was wrong.

Between the two men existed a liking, a friendship, as deep as it was rare. The regulations here were not too severe; they could talk at will, Manning could have his brushes and sketches, Cotterel could have his books. Yet it was prison. And Manning, who had acted from his experience as buffer for this younger man, who had saved him repeatedly from errors of impulse and passion and despair, could sense that some new crisis was upon them.

It came out one evening when, the recreation period over, they were back in their cell together. Cotterel, who had been silent all day, suddenly voiced his thought, as they sat side by side.

"I'll be leaving you soon. It's my one regret: that I'll be leaving you."

Manning started slightly, as an inkling of the truth flashed over him. He bent a penetrating regard on the other man, a look of almost terrified questioning. Cotterel's lips twisted in a bitter grimace, and he nodded.

"It's Frenchy Doran," he went on, defiantly. "He's got everything fixed; he's taken me in on it. The break's for tonight, Manning. You needn't argue against it, either. Oh, I know you mean well, you want to save me from any mistakes, but save your breath. This time it's going through. Two can make it; everything's arranged, I tell you."

Manning's uneasiness was frozen into actual terror. He knew Frenchy Doran, and distrusted the man acutely. Why? He could not say. And Cotterel, he perceived, was in no mood for argument.

He did not speak; he could not. Manning was dumb. Slowly his hand lifted. He began to speak with his fingers. In these long months, he had taught Cotterel the language of the dumb, and Cotterel had become fluent in it. Now, with his deft, slender fingers, the artist-forger made words.

"My friend, I sha'n't argue against it; I shall only wish you luck, now and ever. What argument could I use? I have none. I can only say to you, what Mary Fallon said to her lover, Johnson the smuggler."

His hands fell. Cotterel frowned a little and looked up.

"Eh? Who was Johnson?"

"A rather famous fellow who had quarters in the Fleet Prison in London, a hundred and thirty-five years ago—in 1802. A daring, desperate man who had served his country with such heroism that he was pardoned; then he resumed smuggling, was caught, was clapped into Fleet Prison, and was facing a death-sentence. You know, they executed a man for almost anything in those days. And Johnson, who had been about to

marry this Mary Fallon, was jerked to prison almost from the altar."

COTTEREL GAVE him a wary glance. "Yes? And what was it the girl said to him?"

Manning's gray and wrinkled features did not reflect his inward fear and anxiety. He knew better than to betray it. But the very name of Frenchy Doran made his heart contract.

"Something vitally true in all life, Cotterel," came the reply from his long fingers, from his earnest gaze. "Something true now, this very minute; and yet rather difficult to understand."

"One of your psychic notions?" Cotterel smiled as he spoke, not with ridicule but with affection.

Manning shook his head.

"No; nothing mysterious or hidden, and yet not easy to grasp without knowing all the circumstances. It's a grim and ugly yarn, but damned heroic all the same. As you know, Fleet Prison was reserved for debtors, and Johnson had been put there for his debts, while the more serious case was being prepared. He was a desperate fellow who stopped at nothing—young, rash, impulsive, with clear brave eyes and a stout heart. Just the type to fall into some rascal's trap. Your really heroic man gets taken in by a smooth tongue, most of the time."

MANNING PAUSED, not attempting to point his words in the least. He knew that Frenchy Doran had one of the slickest tongues going. He was sure that Cotterel was in a trap, but he did not say so. He was a wise old chap, shrewd, remarkably intelligent, and this young fellow had become like a son to him.

His fingers began to move again. He spoke of Johnson, and the historic old Fleet Prison, close to Fleet Market—a landmark of ancient London, where many a famous man had been housed for debt. Johnson's cell, with a tiny barred window, was in the very heart of the prison. They were taking no chances with this man, whose reckless and desperate character was well known. Johnson had even vowed publicly that he would never remain caged up to be hanged or deported.

He was given liberty enough—a daily walk in the court, communication with other prisoners or visitors. And today he had a visitor, who came upon him as he was talking with Jem Daly. A "flash" gentleman was Jem, glib of tongue, and suave of manner, and resting here for a burden of debt that would have dismayed many a heartier man.

Mary Fallon came upon the two of them in the "yard," and Johnson introduced his companion, who thoughtfully left the two of them alone. A loitering guard kept his eye on them to see that the girl passed over no contraband article, but remained out of earshot.

If Mary Fallon was not lovely, she had a true, fine eye, and the inner beauty that comes from a clean true heart; she could see under the skin of a man, and if she found great things in the smuggler whom she loved, she could also find less noble qualities in men who were of better repute. It was no harm to be a smuggler in those days, when half Sussex and Devon was in on the game.

Johnson held her hands and looked into her eyes, and it was well that the guard could not hear the words his gay laugh concealed.

"Tomorrow night and each night, my dear," said he, "be waiting with a coach and four at the end of the Fleet Market. Write to my old partner at Brighton, George Huntley; tell him to have his lugger ready, hanging off and on the cove we know at midnight of each night. I'll signal him with four lantern-flashes."

The eyes of the girl dilated, her cheeks paled.

"No!" she exclaimed. "You—oh, do you mean it?"

"Faith, and I do, my dear!" Johnson laughed eagerly, confidently, and pressed her hands. "Tomorrow night if a chance offers; if not, the first night it does."

"But how on earth have you managed it?" she said, staring at him. "Why, only two days ago you said there was no hope, that the very thought of escape was out of the question, that no one had ever escaped from this dreadful place—"

"That was two days ago," and Johnson chuckled. "I've made a friend, my dear; the man you just now met. He has friends, influence, powerful connections. His own escape is all arranged. He's taking me in with him,"

"That man?" The girl drew back. Her clear gaze clouded. "No—please! Don't have anything to do with him. Don't join him in any escape."

"Eh?" Johnson was astonished. "You'd rather see me swing?"

"Don't be absurd. I'd not want to see you involved with him, however."

"Why? Jem Daly's all right, isn't he?"

SHE SHOOK her head. "I think not. I've no reason to feel this way—"

"Then forget it, my dear," cut in Johnson briskly. "Look you, it's a bargain for one and the other. He gets me out of here, has it all arranged. In return, I get him across to France in Huntley's lugger. Mind you get the word to Huntley—you have his address in Brighton, in care of the Crown & Bells."

"Still I don't like it," said Mary Fallon. "I don't know the man; I don't need to know him. I tell you, don't trust him! I'll not send word to Huntley, unless you promise me here and now not to mention him or the lugger to this man."

Johnson's brows drew down. His rugged, vigorous features were angry.

"Very well; I promise. I'll guarantee him passage, that's all. And now, in the name of heaven—why? What have you got against him? You don't even know him."

"I've seen him. Why, you ask? Perhaps because I love you; and perhaps—" The girl hesitated. Then:

"The heart has its reasons," she said earnestly, "which reason cannot understand. I can't explain, my dear; I can't argue with you. I've no words. I can just feel that this man isn't to be trusted."

"I'll prove that you're wrong," and Johnson laughed again. Then, as the guard approached with word that time was up, he kissed her quickly, and saw her away with a smile.

He laughed to himself whenever he thought of her words. Not trust Jem Daly? Why, it was on him that Daly's safety depended! Daly could manage the job here in London; but

"I don't need to know the man," said Mary
Fallon; "I tell you, don't trust him!"

getting out of England was another thing. Only Johnson could do this—the smuggler who knew every lugger, every skipper, every hidden cove, along the coast. Not trust Jem Daly? Stuff and nonsense!

Yet, now and again, he thought of her strange words: *"The heart has its reasons, which reason cannot understand."*

Next day he met Jem Daly, who asked about the lugger.

"Leave that to me," and Johnson winked. "All set, my lad; the moment we're out of these cursed walls, the job's in my hands. It'll go off like a rope in a greased block, be sure of that. When do we move? Tonight?"

Jem Daly shook his head. "No; we can't spring the trap tonight. The rope ladder's not ready. It's set for tomorrow night, an hour before midnight. The rear wall's the place. That cursed front wall over Fleet Street is seventy feet high—too high. The other's only forty."

For an instant Johnson was seized with dismay. He had told Mary Fallon to wait near Fleet Market, which adjoined the far wall of the prison. However, this would not matter. If he and Daly got over the prison wall at the rear, they could circle around into Fleet Street and so gain the coach. Thus, he said nothing about where the girl was to await them—no use causing trouble, he thought. Besides, Jem Daly came in with a puzzled question.

"What about your cell? Are you sure you can force out the inner panel?"

"Aye, damme, sure! I tried it this morning," said Johnson. "Not the outer one, however. And if you can't get any keys for the two doors, you'll have to force the outer panel—it can be forced inward, but not outward."

"I can do that, right enough," said Daly, and eyed the slim-waisted figure of the smuggler with envy. "Sink me if I don't believe you can get out through those holes! It's more than I could do. Then, you'll be listening for the crunch of the panel?"

Johnson nodded. "Right. Where's the rope ladder to be given us?"

"Rolled up and thrown over the wall, a few minutes before eleven. That's another reason it must be the rear wall—the front one's too high for 'em to throw it over. And further," added Daly, "if we went over the front, we'd have a watchman to think about in Fleet Street. There's none at the rear."

Johnson assented, but it occurred to him that Jem Daly was finding a lot of reasons to tackle that rear wall, when the one fact of its height was reason enough.

When he was locked into his cell for the night, it was his own impatience which operated, curiously enough, to reveal the frightful gin of treachery laid so invitingly before his path.

His cell, or rather room, had an inner and an outer door, set with different locks to make it doubly certain that the inmate would stay put. Those locks, also, were expressly designed to obviate any effort at picking them. It was confidently asserted that this was the most escape-proof cell in the entire prison. The man inside, however, invariably has sharper eyes than the man outside.

Johnson had observed one thing forgotten, or never known, by anyone else. Above the doors had originally been set a pane of glass, the width of the door and some eight inches high. In each instance, the glass had been replaced, no doubt at some far distant date, with a panel of wood. The panels had been applied by a workman elevated between the two doors. The innermost, cracked with age, could be forced from within the cell, as Johnson had found to his own satisfaction. The outer panel, however, could not be attacked with any success except from outside, since it must be forced inward. Thus, with the help of a confederate, Johnson might hope at least to leave his cell. When Jem Daly had broached the idea of an escape, it was at once evident to Johnson that he was as good as free—in which Daly concurred.

Now, when he was locked in for the night, Johnson reflected impatiently that he might not hear the crunch of the outer panel when Daly forced it, unless he first sprung the inner panel. A turnkey would look in on him at ten o'clock and take away his light; but he could force the panel a bit now without any risk that it would be noticed, and accordingly he went to work.

DRAWING HIS stool to the door, he mounted it. He had no tools, but required none for this job, the panel being split and warped with age. Johnson put his weight against it, hammered with the ball of his fist, and the nails gave until the panel, at the top, was out a good inch and ready to fall away at one hearty shove. Satisfied, Johnson descended from the stool, took it back to the table, and picking up a quill, began to compose a letter.

This letter was addressed to the chief jailer, and detailed in proper impudence the entire scheme of his escape—without mentioning Daly. When he had finished it, Johnson perused it with a chuckle and tucked it out of sight.

It was nearly ten o'clock when the chief jailer and turn-key appeared, took a cursory look around, removed the light, and departed. The inner door was locked. Then, as the turnkey fumbled for his keys at the outer door, Johnson heard a laugh, and the voice of the chief jailer.

"Keep away from here the rest of the night, Jarge. If ye hear noises, be deaf. It's a break for liberty—the hard'un inside there goes over the back wall, and into the arms of the sojers. It's bullets he'll get—"

Johnson stiffened incredulously to the snatch of talk. He heard more; a cold hand clutched at him. The voices came clearly enough through the gap he had made in the panel. Before the two men closed the outer door and departed, he had heard what made him weak and sick—positively sick. He had never before come to close grips with black treachery; he had never guessed there could be such vileness behind a mask of comradely friendship.

JEM DALY had not only split on him, but was taking him over that rear wall to be shot down or caught in the act of escape—probably to be crippled and hanged.

They were afraid of him.... They wanted to be rid of him. And Jem Daly was getting money for it, and a free pardon. No doubt whatever of all this, since each detail of the escape was known, even to the rope ladder measured to fit the rear wall. No one else could have peached. Daly was the man!

In his agony of spirit, in his terror, in his bitter burning fury, Johnson all of a sudden lifted his head. He remembered the words of Mary Fallon; he could comprehend them now.

"So, you dog, you'd peach—and turn me in for money, would you!"

"The heart has its reasons—" Aye! In happier days he had marveled at how she could read a man for good or bad. Now, in his eagerness, he had forgotten this, had refused to admit there could be anything to her distrust of Daly. Well, she had been dead right. It was an old trick. He had heard of it more than once; to turn in another prisoner and be rewarded for it. No wonder Daly had been so anxious to get everything out of his mind except that rear wall; the Judas was making delivery there!

Johnson began to pace up and down his room. Little by little, his tumult of mind quieted. Settle with Daly? Yes, by God! But that was not all. He caught at the farther thought, juggled it, turned it to his purpose in a fervor of hope. Why not, indeed?

Why not swing the whole damned treacherous scheme to work his actual escape?

He sank down on his cot and stared into the darkness. Undoubtedly, no one would be watching that front wall—that seventy-foot wall. A rope ladder made for a forty-foot wall would not reach, of course. But he remembered, now; ten feet above the street, on the blank face of that front wall, were street lights. They were placed on immensely solid iron brackets embedded in the wall and projecting four or five feet. Good! If he could reach one of those, the distance was cut to sixty feet.

A forty-foot rope ladder for a sixty-foot descent? Hardly. Then, suddenly, Johnson leaped to his feet. Jem Daly had a knife, had boasted of having it, only today. A rope ladder has two sides. Take twenty feet of rope from one side, attach it to the other side with the deft skill of a seaman—and it becomes sixty feet over all. Twenty feet of ladder, at the top. Forty more feet of line, which any seaman could descend hand over hand, even bumping into a wall as he descended! Well, it would be no child's play either, but—

"I can do it if any man can!" muttered Johnson, clenching and flexing his hands in the darkness. "I can do it, turn the tables on 'em all, and make it safely! If by any chance they have sojers waiting in front—well, I'll run that risk. It's not likely. They depend on that rat Jem Daly to lead me into the trap."

At thought of Daly, he flexed his hands again; strong hands, hot with the flame of rage that rose in his heart.

And then, upon his decision, came the crunch and splinter of wood. The outer panel was being forced. There, at least, Jem Daly was keeping his word. Fast, then, fast! Act, before they surmised anything amiss with their bloody treachery!

Johnson stripped to shirt and breeches. In savage haste, he pulled his stool to the door and mounted on it; his fist knocked out the loosened panel. The two doors were close together, were indeed almost a double door. From close ahead came another crunch as the other panel was forced in. He reached through to it, caught it, and tore the wood clear. The voice of Daly came to him in a guarded word.

"Johnson?"

"Aye," he rejoined, and started through the double opening, arms first.

IT WAS a struggle. Twice he thought himself stuck and done for; but each time he tore himself through and on. When at last he was in the clear, and with a final heave and twist let himself go for the fall, Daly was there to give him a helping hand.

Johnson came to his feet with a growl.

"Let's have that knife of yours."

Jem Daly thrust it into his hand in the darkness. Johnson pocketed it—and then he had the other man by the throat, holding him in a grip of steel.

"So, you dog, you'd peach—and turn me in for money, would you! I know the whole thing. Rear wall, says you, and the sojers waiting there to take me—and you with a pardon and a purse of guineas. How much are they paying you? Speak up!"

He relaxed his grip slightly. Jem Daly tore at his arms with ineffectual fingers, and gasping words escaped him.

"Twenty guineas—and—and I had to do it—"

"You don't have to do it now," said Johnson, and clamped in his fingers before Jem Daly could get out a scream.

There was the confession, had he needed any, to sink his iron grip into that throat. He clung, while Daly's struggles grew weaker and ceased, and the man went limp. Then Johnson flung him aside, careless whether he lived or died, and slipped out into the "yard."

A few dim lights burned feebly. There were no guards; the prisoners were locked in each night, and this sufficed. Grudging each moment of delay, Johnson sped for the rear of the place. It was all dark here under the wall; he suppressed an oath as he began to fumble and peer about. He realized for the first time what a task he had set himself without a light—to find a bundle that had somehow been hurled over that wall. Or perhaps it had merely been left somewhere, by a turnkey in on the scheme.

Minutes passed. Desperately, he began to quarter the ground, in panic lest there be no ladder at all and his whole plan gone flittering. That meant he would be taken for murder, if Jem Daly were dead.

HIS FOOT caught on something hard that tripped him. He felt for it, and his fingers came on the curved prong of a grapnel, then upon ropes snaking across the stones. With a heart-leap, he gathered up the grapnel, the rope ladder; a burst of relief that was almost beyond endurance drew a gasp from his lips. He trembled with the swift transition from despair to hope. Then, turning, he headed for the front of the prison. Stairs, and the top of that high wall!

Seventy feet—it seemed a frightful, incredible gap to bridge, as he craned from the edge and looked down. But there below him the lights glimmered; the street was empty; there was no clump of booted heels. He must take the risk of passers-by while he was descending, and of the watch. He had no idea of the time; he did not know when the watch came by.

With the knife, he worked swiftly. He armed out one of the side ropes, guessing at the three-foot lengths; twenty feet of it. Then he cut it, and made his splice, and a better splice he never made. His life depended on this one.

It was all done, at length. He crept along the wall until he came directly above one of those lights on their iron brackets. The bracket would hold him, all right; just such brackets had held many an aristocrat in Paris, ten years back, when the mob swung up their victims *"à la lanterne."* He made fast the grapnel, waited for one last moment to peer down and listen. Nothing there but emptiness and silence. Good! The ladder went down, the single rope below it.

THEN, TO his horror, Johnson saw that something was wrong; the rope was short of the bracket. He stared down for an instant, took a deep breath, and reached his legs forward. Short?

No matter for that. He could drop to the bracket, drop again to the street. The bracket, in fact, was wide and stout; he could even drop astride of it, with a bit of luck. No backing out now!

Aware that those street-lamps lit up the whole face of the wall, Johnson wasted no time in his descent. He came to the ladder's end, got the single rope below in between his feet, and went on down, hand over hand. It was no child's play, as he had warned himself. He swung and humped against the wall until he had to cling there in frantic effort and wait for the motion to stop.

The glare of light from below crept closer. He paused and looked down, judging his distance, his chances. Not so bad, after all! The rope was short, but he could hang by his hands from the very end of it and almost touch the bracket with his feet. Yes, no trick at all to drop astride of it, and no time to spend doing it, either.

He went on. His feet were past the rope's end now. He lowered himself carefully to the very limit, swung with his back to the wall, poised himself there, and looked down. The dazzling lamp blinded him for an instant. Then he could see the bracket clearly. Yes, he could make it without trouble—

"Past eleven o'the clock, and all's well! Past eleven o'the clock, and all's well!"

Cold sweat broke out upon him. The voice was down there, not thirty feet away; the voice, and a shuffle of feet. A watchman, crying the hour, coming past the prison. And he here on the rope, clinging with his hands, unable to cling long, hanging in plain sight on the wall!

Already poised, he let go abruptly. It was a short fall; he caught the bracket as he landed astride. Exactly as he had figured, his shoulders came back against the wall and stayed him from any overbalance. He was secure.

And upon this, a low gasp of agony rose to his lips; he checked it there. Terror clutched at him, the frightful realization of a hurt all but mortal. He put a hand to the iron-work on which he was poised. His fingers found what he had failed to see—a sharp projection of iron. Frantically, he clutched at his thigh; the whole length of it was torn, from knee almost to the hip, horribly torn by that projection. The blood was spurting, seeping through his fingers as he held cloth and flesh together in a supreme effort.

For, almost directly below, the watchman was shuffling along.

"Past eleven o' the clock, and all's well!"

A ghastly grin contorted the lips of Johnson. Why, the dark blood was dripping almost on the man below! But the figure passed on, never glancing up or around, the monotonous voice ringing out and lessening. Even had the watchman looked up, those lights would possibly have dazzled him.

O N E   L A S T, terrible exertion, and Johnson swung himself over the bracket, hung by his hands, and dropped. It took all his nerve, all his iron will; when he struck, it was with a rush of agony that wrenched a groan from him.

He stirred, moved, came to his feet. No soldiers here; all was well. But when he tried to walk, he collapsed. His leg was soaked in blood. New terror took hold on him, lest he bleed to death, lest his strength flow out. Desperate, he dragged himself along below the wall, teeth grimly set.

He forgot, however, that some one who was no enemy had been awaiting him.

She came suddenly, running, a man's figure following her. With low cries of pity, of tenderness, she was helping him; the man lent a hand. Johnson, between them, was staggering toward the waiting coach and four. Near the last light, he ordered a stop; the terrible wound must be bandaged before his life flowed out. He stretched himself on the stones, ripped off his shirt, and the driver of the coach tied up the ripped flesh, tied it hard and stoutly.

Then they went on again, and were gone—off for Brighton and the secret cove, and the lugger of Huntley bound for France and safety!

The prisoner of the Fleet had escaped.

SO, WITH the end of his story, Manning's slender, artistic hands drooped and his long fingers were still. He glanced sideways at Cotterel. The younger man was sitting with a frown of absorption. He looked up, and a queer ugly light was stirring in his eyes.

"You know, Manning, I've always had a lot of respect for your hunches," he said abruptly, almost as though he had not been listening to that story at all. "And that's the best definition of a hunch that I ever heard—the heart has its reasons, which reason can't understand! Yep, it's true, too."

Manning nodded, a little wearily. His fingers fluttered again.

"I suppose we'll be saying good-by pretty soon?"

Cotterel merely grunted. After a moment, he made reply.

"I've been wondering about one or two things. Frenchy Doran is pretty thick with one of the screws, for instance. Hm! D'you suppose he'd get a pardon if he spoiled a break?"

"Absolutely."

Cotterel drew a deep breath. All his moody excitement had vanished; he was more like himself again. A smile came to his lips. He turned and met the eyes of Manning, with a long, slow regard.

"I owe you a lot," he said simply. "Just how much, it's hard to realize. No, we're not saying good-by—not tonight, anyhow. Put her there, Manning."

He extended his hand. The older man met it with a quick grip, and Cotterel smiled again.

"The heart has its reasons—yes, I guess that's right. I may kick myself for it—but I'm staying. Let's turn in."

FOUR OUT OF BONDAGE

THE STEADFAST LOYALTY OF MASTER AND DOG JOINS WITH
THE VALOR OF THE HOPELESS TO DRIVE THREE PRISONERS
OF WAR THROUGH A PITILESS PILGRIMAGE.... PERHAPS THE
BEST YET IN THIS FINE SERIES OF "STRANGE ESCAPES."

IN FOR life....

The three words grew and grew in Cotterel's brain. They filled his thoughts, his mind, his will, with a sort of hideous paralysis. He did everything mechanically. Now, back in the cell, he did nothing.

All day he had not responded to a question, had not spoken, had merely stared blankly ahead of him. Now he sat with his face in his hands, unmoving. Manning watched him with concern, with anxiety. Old Manning knew everything that prison does to a man. Even what it does to an innocent man, though the old forger was not innocent by a good deal.

Cotterel, however, was innocent; of this, Manning was convinced.

His grayish features lined and drawn, Manning eyed the younger man, touched him, could evoke no response. Cotterel merely shook his head and refused to look up at the nimble fingers. This was the only way Manning could speak; he was dumb. He was not deaf, however.

Here in this prison life was, comparatively speaking, easy. Cotterel could have books and the older man could have also his own playthings—his sketches, his crayons, his brushes. He turned to them now. Those deft old fingers were not only the fingers of a forger; they were also the fingers of an artist. Criminal though he was, Manning was like many another skilled engraver—a genuine and rare artistic gift was his.

N O W   H E worked rapidly, with his sure, swift strokes. When he had finished, he went over to Cotterel, shook him roughly awake to things around. In front of him, Manning held the sketch. Cotterel focused vague eyes upon it and saw it was the sketch of a dog—a splendid, vigorous Alsatian. He lifted sullen

"I take no chances with vagabonds and gypsies; I know your tricks," said the man. "Bring the dog here."

eyes. "What the hell is this for?" he demanded. "Leave me alone, can't you? I've got all the rest of my life to talk." The hurt look in Manning's eyes shamed him. Besides, he was curious. "Well?" he added quickly. "What's it about? Who's this dog?"

"Azor." Manning spelled the word out on his fingers. He had to spell it twice before Cotterel grasped it as a name.

"Azor? That's a fool name," he commented aloud. "Where did it come from?"

"A man like you," Manning made reply. "You're brooding about being in for life."

"No, for death!" burst out Cotterel violently, then relaxed.

"That's it. Death. That's the thought, the awful thought; here for life and death—all this life is a death. Don't you understand?"

Manning, who understood perfectly all that prison existence inspired in a man, nodded quietly, and leaned forward. He had Cotterel's attention now, which was the thing he most desired. Too well he knew how such a mood as this, unchecked, would end: a sudden frenzy, a maniac attack on a guard, a slash at the wrists with anything to hand. The old forger's abiding horror was that once a cell-mate of his had actually bitten into his arteries, at such a moment.

His affection for Cotterel, which had grown with the long months into a very real regard, guided his silent words as he went on. Cotterel had once loved dogs—a fact of which Manning was not ignorant. Swiftly he formed words:

"You speak of death, Cotterel? Of slow death? You know nothing whatever about it. It's not death which frightens you; it's the waiting for it—right?"

Cotterel groaned.

"Yes. The horror of monotony," he muttered. "The endless torment—"

"And suppose you got away from here, by some miracle?" went on Manning's fingers. "Suppose you had safety within your grasp, within actual sight—nothing would make you turn back?"

"Don't be a fool," snapped the younger man. "We're not talking about anything like that, Manning."

"Nor snow and ice, on naked feet, nor hunger on lean bellies," said Manning. "What do you know of suffering, with your mental horror of monotony? Bah!"

Cotterel scowled. "Never mind about all that sort of thing. Maybe I can't take it; I don't give a hang. What about the dog? What kind of a crazy name was that—Azor?"

"An Austrian name," assented the older man. "Azor, yes. Don't ask me the derivation; I don't know. Azor was one of those animals who seem to have the soul of a man behind their luminous and intelligent eyes. Lieutenant Ellrich had picked up the dog somewhere; Azor stuck to him in camp, in battle, in captivity. Ellrich was an Austrian officer—a man something like you, sympathetic, friendly, a man extremely fond of animals. Needless to say, Azor was devoted to him, with all the solidly centered affection of dog for man in a world gone mad."

"When was all this?" said Cotterel.

"Back in the Napoleonic days." Manning studied him for a moment, then nodded sagely as he went on: "Yes, a man very much like you, young, ardent, and able to endure incredible sufferings. Why? Because of his mental make-up. He was the mental, imaginative type, which can suffer intolerably from anticipation of suffering; yet when it actually comes, can endure all the more for this reason. The brain gives the power to endure; the mind endures, my friend. Such a man hangs on where stronger, stouter, abler men fall miserably and give up. The brain never gives up, in such a man as you."

Cotterel laughed, a little scornfully. Manning nodded at him again.

YES, ELLRICH was just such a man; slender, young, too much strength in his face to be called handsome, perhaps, and overwhelmed by calamity. For Ellrich had become a prisoner of the French, stripped of everything he possessed except old clothes, moved from point to point with other prisoners—to Nice, at length, and then up to Valence.

It was the dead of winter, and he suffered, as prisoners of war suffered in those days.

All the while Azor remained with him. Something in the mien of that splendid dog, in his intelligence, in his utter devotion to Ellrich, touched the hearts of the French. All men admired the dog, and they admired the mutual understanding and love between dog and man. For Azor actually seemed to understand whatever Ellrich said to him.

A dog, perhaps, does not understand man's words—or perhaps he does. Who knows? He understands gestures, a tone of voice, even a look. More than most people realize, a dog watches the eyes of a man and comprehends them—that is to say, an intelligent dog. The ordinary beast may judge only by that strange acid-like emanation from the pores of the skin which is produced when a man hesitates from fear of him; then he snarls and snaps. But the unusual beast, the dog with intelligence, judges more often from the eyes alone. So it was with Azor.

WITH OTHER prisoners, Ellrich was moved up to Valence; two of these prisoners were old friends, brother Hussar officers, Mannheim and Lipnicker by name—both of them young, impulsive, able. At Valence, they found themselves in hell.

The dead of winter, remember. Their prison was the refectory of a former convent. For a bed, they had moldy straw, nothing else, and little of it at that. For garments, they had only the rags left them by the rapacity of their captors. For heat, within these walls of stone, they had nothing at all, except what they could gain by huddling together. For food, they had one loaf of army bread each three days, a handful of beans, a little olive oil; nothing else.

They were tortured by absolute famine, by cold and frost, by utter lack, by constant despair. The belly of Azor grew thin and gaunt; none the less, each of the three spared the dog a little of his meager fare, enough to keep Azor with life in him.

"Have you noticed," said Ellrich one bitter night, as they huddled together, "that these local gendarmes who guard us, these country police, pay almost no heed to what we do? It would be easy to give them the slip."

Lipnicker laughed in hollow misery. "Yes. They know well enough that anyone who got away, would be lost! In the heart of France, without a hope of getting anywhere—"

"Let's chance it!" exclaimed Mannheim. "Right, Ellrich; it can be done! I've traveled all over this part of France, before the war. I know the towns, the highways. We can reach Switzerland and be safe!"

"Not so fast." Ellrich had started something, but he was too shrewd to go blindly at it. "Lipnicker's right. We haven't a cent

Yelling out a hoarse snatch of song, Lipnicker went capering down the road—a grotesque scarescrow come to life.

of money. We've no shoes; nothing but rags bound around our feet. No food. No warm clothes at all. We speak French very badly. Can you imagine any greater odds against our success?"

"Yes, one," said Lipnicker, and ruffled the heavy fur of the dog who lay with them and helped keep them from freezing. "Azor. If he's with us, we'll certainly be recaptured."

"Right," said Ellrich. "Well, I'm for it—and Azor goes with us! Better to die on the road to freedom, than to perish here. If we remain a few more days, we'll have no strength left for the attempt. Make up your minds."

The impetuous Mannheim voted yes. Lipnicker shrugged and voted yes. They talked over every detail. The former convent was on the town outskirts. By leaving after nightfall, their escape would not be discovered until morning.

They voted to try it the following evening....

Morning came. Ellrich wakened, cold and stiff. He felt about for Azor, who always lay against him; there was no dog. Azor had disappeared.

That morning Ellrich was a prey to consternation, terror, grief. The dog was gone, and no one knew anything about him. He could have got out of the almost unguarded convent easily enough, during the night. Despite the snow, he had done so, in fact.

Early in the afternoon he showed up, while the prisoners were at their misery of exercise in the trampled snow of the convent garden. Azor appeared, bounding, vigorous, excited with joy. His belly was rounded again, and clamped between his jaws was a huge well-polished bone.

E L L R I C H   WA S lost between joy and fear. Obviously Azor had been off foraging, and with great success. But as Lipnicker said:

"He may get away with it once, but look out! To these accursed miserly French, meat is like gold and jewels; some town butcher will be in demanding that Azor be shot. Good thing we're pulling out tonight. Knowing he's in enemy country, he's been pillaging—a good Austrian, eh? Better put him on a rope tonight."

Ellrich agreed.

That night a warm, soft snow began to fall. Under its cover the three men scaled the convent wall, unseen. Azor, kicking and struggling, was hauled up on his rope and let down on the other side. The rotten rope broke; no harm done. No more need of it now! Free! It was as simple as that—apparently.

They pushed on hard all night, into the dawn, into the morning. A patch of timber, a fire, and they huddled around it for an hour, then pushed on again until night fell. By this time, fuller realization had come to them: Ellrich's listing of the odds against them had omitted one important fact.

In all the three hundred miles they must cover, not a village, at this time, but had its own post of local police, inspecting all who passed. Without passports, travelers were at once arrested.

The three men and the dog pressed on. Without a sou, they dared not approach any tavern; they dared not enter any town or village. They foraged in the fields, stole what could be found, begged where any house offered refuge. In a week's time they were leaving bloody tracks on the snow and ice.

ANOTHER WEEK passed, and a third; they were past Besançon, halfway to their goal. Not much of a story in that, you might say; and you would be correct. It was, on the contrary, an epic, a vague heroic dream from which the memory of those three men ever afterward recoiled in horror.

Their feet tracked blood in the snow all the time now. What it meant to be warm, they hardly knew, except from labor. Peasants, here and there, gave them labor of sorts, and paid in meager food—labor from which the peasants themselves shrank in distaste. They bedded in the snow, or sometimes, by luck, in hedge-corners or in luxury of straw. Bearded and emaciated, clad in tattered rags, they no longer resembled normal men; they were taken for vagabonds.

Every day was a prolonged agony. If they found any work, they shared it, for among the three of them was now barely the strength of one man. Yet they staggered on, one aiding another. When one broke down completely, the others waited and helped him on. Mannheim they always sent in to beg at a farm. He was the youngest; and if the sight of warmth and shelter and women-folk shattered him, his tears were so pitiful that even a hardened farm-wench occasionally took pity. Where it was safe, they separated and went begging, and thanked God for the alms of a frozen potato or a crust of bread.

Hardest to endure was the snow underfoot, and the bitter cold around. Yet they endured it all, and held on. The country was searched for escaped prisoners, but mere vagabonds were safe.

As for Azor, in this frozen, desolate, well-guarded country

even his hunting ability was set at naught. He followed them, a gaunt skeleton of a dog; but his bodily warmth was enough to keep them from freezing at night.

Besançon passed, the evil road half gone; and now, it seemed, they were at the very end of their ability to keep going. They still had flint and steel, however. When Mannheim fell in a dead stupor of exhaustion, they pulled him out of the road, broke sticks from the trees, and finally got a fire alight. With a rush, a flurry of snow, and a triumphant "Woof!" Azor dug out a frozen, long-dead bird. At the sharp cry of Ellrich, he surrendered the prey without bolting it.

This proof of devotion touched Ellrich deeply.

"My friend, you shall have it; but we must share it with you," he muttered through his frost-cracked lips. Melting snow in a pannikin, he dropped the bird into the water; Lipnicker staggered in with some willow bark; of this they made a horrible brew. When the last drop was shared among them, Ellrich handed the sodden ruin of the little bird to Azor, who downed it at a gulp and muzzled him gratefully.

"S O N O W we're finished," Lipnicker said mournfully, freeing his beard of clogging ice. "We're done; a hundred and fifty miles to go—no use."

Ellrich regarded the two of them with the stark ghost of his merry smile.

"On the contrary, my friends! We've just got our second wind. Here we've dined on stewed pheasant and champagne—let this glorious repast put heart into us all!"

"We can't do the impossible," Mannheim said.

"Why not? We're doing it. Now look here." Ellrich had melted the frozen rags binding his feet. He unwrapped the worn, shredded bits of cloth and laid bare the hideous objects beneath, the things that had been feet. Cracked asunder, bleeding even now, swollen, dark with frozen blood, deformed and almost shapeless.

"A month ago, if you had shown me such things for my feet,

I'd have vomited," he observed. "But now I can regard them without a tremor of emotion. They carry me on; they will carry me farther. I've learned to use them in new ways, to favor them, to make them serve me as well as they ever did. I still have a hundred and fifty miles to go on these ragged stumps of feet—and I can do it. Can't you?"

"No," murmured Mannheim, looking up at the sky with frightened eyes.

"No," said Lipnicker, gnawing at his beard.

"Come along!" Ellrich wrapped up his feet anew and came erect. "Ten miles to cover before darkness comes. That leaves only a hundred and forty. Of course we can do it! Don't listen to what your bodies say, gentlemen. Up with you!

They were mere drifting shadows of men, struggling against stark famine.

Kaiserliks, these French call us; well, show 'em what Kaiserliks can do!"

Under the spur of his words, his action, his personality, they staggered up.

The two of them were like automatons, plodding ahead in dumb, numb agony. With Ellrich it was different; his brain was awake. Anticipation, with such a man, intensifies the thought of pain. Once the pain arrives, the brain has something else to reach forward after. So terrible has been the anticipation, that the reality does not seem bad.

Thus with Ellrich.

All three of them possessed one thing: youth, which can undergo perfectly incredible torments without a scar remaining. Then, there was Azor; the splendid animal had become a friend indeed, one of themselves. As they were reduced to a form of bestial existence, they came down to the level of the dog. Azor suffered too. His ice-choked paws were raw and split and bleeding, like their own; but his great spirit went out to the men who suffered more than he. When one of them fell, Azor crawled to him, muzzled him, licked cold hands and face; when famine griped their bellies, Azor alone made no complaint, always had a wag of the tail, a warm and friendly muzzle, a glow of the eyes that shamed them.

Ellrich pushed them on. Every day was a crisis; every day they accomplished the impossible. They achieved superhuman things. Another week passed, and another; the Swiss frontier was approaching, yet still horribly far away.

In all that time, just one real meal, and this was scanty, when they encountered a band of gypsies—Egyptians, they were called—making an escape from war-filled France. A touch of kindly German speech, a charity of bread and sausage and new rags to replace the old; then the gypsies were gone again, and the four pressed on with new life for a few days.

It was Azor who drew them from death when the snow fell thick and heavy. They had huddled in a hedgecorner, and were

With moaning gulps of joy, Azor
fell at the feet of Ellrich.

covered deeply, sleeping in warmth and oblivion. They would never have wakened, but for Azor. He dug clear, he frisked around them, his great paws uncovered them to the cold sunlight, he dragged Ellrich by the collar. Ellrich came awake, with the dog's teeth nipping his arm.

They were mere drifting shadows of men, struggling against an insuperable barrier of famine. In those days the French themselves suffered bitterly; the men were gone to war; the women remaining at home were suspicious of all strangers or openly hostile. To be stranded in such country as this, without a copper, was the worst fate imaginable.

ONE AFTERNOON the four companions were slogging painfully along when they came slap upon a regiment of French infantry, marching in the opposite direction. Azor gave them warning, but they were all too desperately intent upon mere endurance to give any heed, until too late. The French surrounded them, and questioned them.

Mannheim, whose French was very fair, gave a story of being Swiss watchmakers who had fallen on evil days and were trying to get home. The French were amazed and pitying; but this regiment had come from the upper Rhine country and was absolutely destitute; the uniforms were rags; the food was biscuit rations, and little at that. A pitying *vivandière* gave them each a swig of brandy—an ill deed, though well meant.

The French went on. Before they were out of sight, Lipnicker had gone out of his head—that hearty swig of brandy had finished his senses. He broke from Ellrich and Mannheim. Yelling out a hoarse snatch of song, he went down the road, capering, tossing his arms, a grotesque scarecrow come to life.

They toiled after him. He fought them like a madman when they finally caught up. He broke away once more and capered on, only to plunge headlong into a snowbank as the burst of fiery energy went out of him.

HE WAKENED sane enough, but ill. They were all ill, with that brandy. Ellrich got to his feet, after a brief rest. He kicked the others feebly until they stirred and groaned and moved up erect.

"Keep going! Walk it off!" he rasped, bent almost double with his own griping pain. "March!"

Somehow they managed it, and with darkness sank down again, the evil effects worked off.

Morning, and Ellrich driving them to the road. The bones stuck out of his face; for he, like Azor, was a walking skeleton. His matted, unkempt beard draggled over his chest. He was so weak that he had poor control over his steps, yet he drove them relentlessly, just as he drove himself. His whole power of will was concentrated on one thing alone: to keep moving forward.

Yet there were limits; if not to the will, at least to the power of weakened bodies to respond to this will. It came, when they reached the village of Courtelevant. They could feel death mounting in them; even Ellrich could feel it, could not deny it. A signpost at a crossroads told them the name of the village ahead, and they consulted.

"Courtelevant," mumbled Mannheim, his sunken eyes feverish. "Huningue is still thirty miles ahead, and the frontier. Thirty miles! It's impossible."

"Impossible," assented the cracked, swollen lips of Lipnicker.

Ellrich stared at them, and in his heart echoed the word. Yet his brain recoiled from it.

"We'll have to chance gendarmes and enter this village," he said with a last flicker of energy, "Beg. They can't refuse us."

"No use," said Mannheim. "If they do, we're done. We're done, *done*, I tell you!" His voice rose shrilly, his eyes glared at Ellrich. "I'm dying; I can feel it. The pain's all gone. I'm just too weak to move. I can't even make the village, there."

"Make it," said Ellrich. "If we're arrested, well and good; at least, prisoners aren't starved to death. If we have any luck at all, if we get even a few scraps, we can do the last thirty miles."

"Scraps? There are none," mumbled Lipnicker. "These French have no garbage. They eat everything themselves, I'm done too."

Ellrich was done also, and knew it. That final thirty miles bulked before them like a vast gulf. For six weeks they had pressed on, and now it was the end. They could not possibly go beyond this village. Even to reach the village, was agony intolerable.

They went on. Azor trailed them. His head was hanging, and he limped, now on one leg, now on another; he was the picture of dejection, his ribs showing.

On into the village, careless at last of questions or police. By a miracle, they encountered none at all. The gendarmes had been withdrawn, merged into the local conscription unit for the army. There was none to molest them as they separated to undertake the miserable begging job from door to door.

THEY WENT through the village from end to end. Ellrich kept Azor with him, naturally. They toured the shops, the houses. Mannheim turned on his nearly exhausted supply of tears. Lipnicker mumbled his broken, shattered pleas. Ellrich voiced his desperate appeal and pointed to the starving dog.

All in vain. The village larders were too low; every crust, to these peasants, was valuable. The vagabonds were brushed aside, with curses and threats. A number of women gathered and took their brooms to Mannheim, chasing the tottering, emaciated figure down the street.

The three gathered in hopeless misery. One house alone remained. Ellrich had not attempted it; on the doorstep sat a hard-eyed old fellow puffing at a pipe and eying the vagabonds without love, a stout cudgel across his knees.

"Nothing," said Mannheim, and Lipnicker echoed the word with a dry sob.

Ellrich knew it was the end, for all of them. There still remained the man on the doorstep. Smashing down his pride, Ellrich staggered toward him, with Azor at his heels. He came to a halt.

"For the love of God, give us something to eat! A crust, garbage, anything at all," he quavered. "Can't you see we're starving, actually starving? We've eaten nothing in the past twenty-four hours—nothing, I tell you!"

"We have our own troubles here, vagabond," spat out the man, scowling over his pipe as the other two desperate men joined Ellrich.

"But we'll work; we'll do anything!" cried Ellrich in despair.

"Like enough," said the man grimly. "Escaped felons, that's what you are; perhaps prisoners of war, by your accent. Germans or Austrians, eh? If there were any police here, you'd have an answer quick enough. But I tell you what I will do."

ELLRICH WAITED, trembling, watching the man intently.

"That's a good-looking dog you have. I'll buy him from you; I'll give you a good price for him too, in food and money."

Ellrich recoiled. "Sell him? As soon sell you my right arm—nay, rather!" he exclaimed indignantly.

"Then be off with you before I take my stick to you!" And the hard-eyed old fellow puffed at his pipe as he spoke. "You rascally vagabonds! If you were as hard-pressed as you claim, you'd sell the dog quick enough. I like his looks. I can make something of him. Well, make up your minds about it!"

He went into the house and came out, bringing a loaf of bread, a hunk of cheese, and a dozen copper coins—sous. These he set on the doorstep, and waited. Here was the price of Azor.

Ellrich looked at his two companions. His own strength, his will, was gone. This last twenty-four hours had finished him. He thought of the thirty miles ahead, and the heart sank in him. He could not do it; he knew it. He looked at the others. Mannheim, with sunken cheeks and red-rimmed, inflamed eyes, had a ghastly air.

"Do it, for God's sake," Mannheim urged brokenly. "I'm at the last gasp. Refuse, and I'm done. I'll tell them who I am, and let them take me."

Ellrich looked at Lipnicker. The latter was chewing his beard, gazing at the bread and cheese with avid, feverish eyes. He glanced at Ellrich.

"Do it, do it! Don't be a fool. It's no longer a question of keeping on, but of life or death to us."

Ellrich looked at Azor. The dog, too, was staring at the food, his tongue trembling at his chops. Then, suddenly, Mannheim touched the right chord.

"At least, Azor will have food. If you refuse, he'll die with us."

Ellrich broke. Tears in his eyes, tears glittering on his frost-bitten cheeks, he went to Azor, fondled the dog's head, then suddenly turned to the waiting man.

"Agreed," he said hoarsely. "The dog is yours."

"Wait!" The purchaser called to his wife. She came out, bringing a length of heavy chain. "I'll take no chances with vagabonds and gypsies; I know your tricks. Bring the dog here."

Ellrich, his heart in his throat, called Azor and held him while the chain was fastened. Then, clutching the bread and cheese and money, he started away, the other two trailing him.

Azor looked after them. None of the three turned, until they were out of sight. Then they halted. And as they did so, a long, lugubrious howl reached them, a dismal howl of affectionate dismay and farewell. Ellrich dropped the food, stopped his ears, and broke into a run. At the third step, he swayed, fell.

The others pulled him up. They shared a little bread and cheese, and hastened on. The food gave them life, but they dared eat only a little. Twice more, from a distance, the dismal voice of Azor reached them; then it fell silent.

ON, NOW, and on. At every mile they halted, took another bite or so, and went on anew. Ellrich staggered on like a man in stupor, staring straight ahead of him, in his face a frightful bitterness. When the others tried to rouse him, he snarled.

"Judas, at least, had a rope on which to hang himself. I have none. Come on, come on! There's liberty ahead. Keep going!"

His bitter mockery stung them. They broke into angry dissension—their first real quarrel in all those six weeks of hell. The food was putting new heart, new life, into them.

Hours passed. The thirty miles fell behind them, step by step. That one meal had made new men of them all. From a hillock, as evening approached, they saw spires and clock-towers glittering in the sunset.

"Basle!" cried out Mannheim. "Switzerland—freedom!"

A CHOKED cry escaped Lipnicker. They embraced one another. Tears ran down their cheeks. They hugged Ellrich—but they fell away from his glittering eyes, his harsh unchanged features, his wild voice.

"Go on, go on to Basle and welcome!" he said. "Listen! Do you hear it? That's Azor's voice. He's howling still, after all this time—"

"Ellrich! He's ten leagues away!" exclaimed Lipnicker. "For the love of God, keep your head—don't imagine things!"

The sunken, glittering eyes of Ellrich dwelt upon him.

"I'm not mad. I tell you, I hear him calling! I'm going back, that's all. You two go ahead. I'm turning back."

"But why, you fool?" demanded Mannheim. "You can do no good. We've sold the dog. You can't get him back."

"I'm going back to him," said Ellrich resolutely, calmly. "I'll do my best to get him; I'll work it out for that man, pay him back somehow. No arguments, my friends! I've quite settled it with myself. No matter what it costs, I'm going back. I want Azor to know that I didn't desert him, that I'm worth his affection. Even if the worst happens, this knowledge will be a compensation. It will console me."

Lipnicker gasped. "You care what a dog thinks?"

"With all my heart," said Ellrich quietly.

A gesture of farewell. Then he turned and went back the way they had come, giving no heed to their implorant voices.

They looked at each other, and shrugged helplessly. The tattered figure of Ellrich went on, never glancing around. They realized that he had indeed left them, for good, at all costs.

Suddenly, they saw him halt.

A sound lifted on the air, and made them exchange startled glances. They recognized the voice of Azor—no lugubrious howl now, but a swift, exultant, deep-throated bay of gladness. They had heard his voice too often to mistake it. From Ellrich burst a wild, vibrant cry. And then Azor came into sight.

He was running, but not as they had ever seen him run; this time it was more like a sidewise lope. The two men hurried to rejoin their comrade. The dog came on, with his clumsy, staggering run; a sharp yelp made reply to Ellrich's voice, then he forged on in silence. Tongue hanging, eyes afire, body straining, he too was evidently at the last gasp. Then, as they came together, the three men saw the reason.

Behind Azor dragged a full four feet of the heavy chain that had bound him. All this thirty miles, he had dragged the weight with his weakened forces, until, with quick little moaning gulps of joy, he fell at the feet of Ellrich.

The Austrian knelt, embraced him passionately, and while the whining dog licked his hands and face, set free the wire fastening of the chain. It fell into the snow, and Azor surged about him delightedly.

That night they slipped across the frontier, and morning found them in Basle—new men, resting in luxury at the Stork Tavern.

MANNING'S FINGERS ceased their movement. His story was finished. Cotterel, held oblivious of himself, drew a deep breath.

"What a story! What a dog! And by God, what a man!" he broke out, his eyes shining.

Manning smiled. "And a true story, my friend, true in every detail," he went on. "Mind you, it's more than a dog-and-man story. It's the tale of the brain insuperable—the brain, the will, the intellect that drives the body past all bodily endurance. When the end is reached, with such a man, the horizon is lifted and he goes on and on—"

"Tell me!" Cotterel leaned forward eagerly. "How do you know about the story? Who told it to you?"

Manning actually chuckled. "Well, it was handed down to me. Mannheim, in later years, came to America and settled here. His son changed the name to Manning. You see?"

"I see," said Cotterel soberly, staring at the man, the one man, who was his friend.

THE PRISONER OF TOULON

THIS FIFTH OF MR. KEYNE'S DRAMATIC STORIES OF STRANGE
ESCAPES SHOWS US A MAN IN DEADLY PERIL WHO HAD THE RARE
GIFT OF DOING THE RIGHT THING AT THE RIGHT INSTANT.

FOR DAYS, Cotterel had been irritable, excitable, given to flying off at strange tangents. A felon condemned to spend the rest of his life behind the bars cannot, perhaps, be expected to maintain a stoic calm; and yet Cotterel's actions worried his cell-mate deeply.

Old Manning, who shared his cell and his life in prison, was a shrewd observer and a very real friend. In the months since Cotterel had come here, a mutual affection had sprung up between them. Repeatedly, Manning had interposed his own knowledge and skill and sage wisdom, to save the younger man from beating himself against the bars, literally and figuratively. And now he saw breakers ahead, unless Cotterel could be brought to see some reason.

"The trouble with you is that you can't forget you were unjustly condemned," he said, as they sat in the cell together, and Cotterel glowered. "You lack poise."

"Poise be damned!" Cotterel spoke aloud.

Manning, who could not speak aloud, who could not utter a sound, smiled gently at him and went on:

"A lifer, and innocent; that's what burns. Well, forget it, Cotterel! You're still dreaming of escape. What chance have you, in your present frame of mind? None. If you're really bent on escape, I'll help you; but not until you—"

"You'll help me? You mean that?" Cotterel was electrified. He leaned forward, a wild light in his eyes. "Manning, you mean it?"

"Of course," said the nimble fingers of the man who could not speak, the older man whose vocal cords were paralyzed. At the gesture of those fingers, Cotterel drew a deep breath and sat back, staring.

"But," pursued Manning, "not in your present frame of mind. You should take a lesson from Vidocq."

"Who in hell's Vidocq?" snapped Cotterel testily.

Manning smiled. He was no hardened gun-swift criminal, but an artist who had forged the best imitation of government engraving yet seen. He knew everything; particularly, he had made a study of prisons and escapes. Cotterel, ignoring his own question, leaned forward with swiftly flying fingers; in these months of prison, he had learned the knack of it, though Manning was not deaf at all.

"You're in earnest? You'll really help me to escape?" he demanded again.

Manning assented: "Yes."

"Then it's as good as done!" Cotterel exulted, only to frown afresh. "And all this while, you've warned me against escape, you've stopped me from any break—"

"There is more than one kind of escape, my friend," said Manning, rather obscurely. Cotterel could never be certain just what his utterances signified. "Remember, I'll help you only on the one condition: that you get yourself, your brain, in shape. It'll take time. The peculiar thing about Vidocq was that he

never lost his head. He was always, in the most acute crises, cool and well-poised and alert. This quality caused him to escape repeatedly from the worst prisons in France."

"France!" repeated Cotterel…."Who was this fellow Vidocq?"

"The perfect type of rascal."

"Huh! When did he live?"

"A hundred years ago and more, much more."

"Why the devil," exclaimed Cotterel petulantly, "do your yarns nearly always go back so far?"

"For the best reason in the world," Manning rejoined. "It was a period of upheaval, of chaos. It is at such times that men do the most unusual, the most heroic, the most startling actions. They fling aside all inhibitions of law and custom, and become super-human. Scoundrels become great men, like Barras or Talleyrand.

"It is a peculiar thing, too," he went on reflectively, "that at such times the most important things are lost to sight, the less important emerge. Look at General Menou: He lost an army and an empire for France; he was a renegade, became a Turk, maintained a harem, and died disgraced and futile. Yet it was to Menou that France owes her present tri-color, a fact quite unknown today!" Cotterel made an impatient gesture.

"I'm not interested in all that balderdash…. Forgive me, old chap," he added contritely, "but I'm in no mood for it, that's all. I've no patience—"

"No poise, exactly as I said." And Manning smiled again. "You see? You must become like Vidocq; that is indispensable. When he made his escape from the most dreaded prison in France, the galleys of Toulon, it was by a perfect triumph of mental equipoise; it was a blend of careful preparation and actual wit, yes; but in the end the only thing that saved him was his cool shrewdness. When everything was lost, this quality carried him through. Without this quality, you couldn't escape from here."

"Not even with your help?" Cotterel demanded.

"Unless you have it, I'll not give my help!" Manning shook his head. "The perfect escape is rare; it is, nearly always, due to this supreme quality, which enables a man to do the right thing at the right instant—no matter what he is called upon to do. The more you examine this statement, Cotterel, the broader and more essential it appears. The right thing at the right time, remember—no matter what it is! Really, it's a tremendously comprehensive statement."

Cotterel smiled, a little wistfully. "I'm no great shucks, I guess," he said. "But I'll do my best, Manning; that much I can promise. I don't get this essential quality of yours; I don't quite savvy what it is. Haven't I got brains?"

Manning relaxed. He had what he most desired, now—the attention of his companion. He knew that he could handle Cotterel, once he could get those inflamed and congested lobes of the brain eased—those lobes which dealt only with the horror of life imprisonment. If he could stimulate other lobes to work, as he had done, half the battle was won. And now to keep them at work.

"You've got everything," he replied. "You'll savvy better when you hear about Vidocq and the galleys. Slavery in the galleys had disappeared, but the name remained for the prison to which the worst and most dangerous criminals were condemned—the prison of Toulon, a sort of Devil's Island of that period, only indescribably worse. Vidocq was no heroic figure, comprehend. He was a rogue, an arrant rogue—"

He broke off and sat for a moment or two in reflection, as though seeking words in which to describe his man; then his slender old fingers began again.

VIDOCQ, TRULY, was no heroic figure. He was just the opposite—so unimpressive, so ordinary and undistinguished in any way, as quite to escape observation. He was the perfect type of person whom you look at in the street and fail to see. And in this fact lay his adeptness at all sorts of rascality.

For, behind this exterior, his brain was quick and cold and sharp as a dagger. Like one of those Corsican daggers, tapering from all sides to a needle-point, whose penetrating power is incredible, until experienced.

DOUBLE IRONS were riveted to Vidocq, by wrist and ankle. With the other "desperate" characters, he lay aboard a floating hulk off the arsenal, which had replaced the galleys of other days. None of this gang was ever sent to work, lest some opportunity for escape be found at the harbor; all were chained day and night to their places, with bare planks for beds, consumed by vermin, and exhausted by the brutal treatment of the prison guards, who delighted in tormenting them.

They were allowed no exercise whatever. Their food was a bare sufficiency to keep a man alive. Aged from fourteen to sixty,—Vidocq was twenty-four,—they were a group of the most hardened murderers and brutes imaginable, given over to the most vicious conversation and acts the human form could compass.

In this hell, Vidocq was placed for life—and by grim irony, for a crime of which he happened to be innocent. However, repeated escapes, and attempts to escape, had made him a marked man.

The convicts were chained in pairs. Vidocq's companion in misery was one Jossas, a merry and genial philosopher, who had posed as a marquis and made friends everywhere, chiefly among the ladies. Jossas was no novice at prison life, or escapes either. He gave Vidocq the best of advice and help.

"Never be in a hurry," he would say complacently. "If you make a break and fail, you get an extra three years; or a lifer like you gets beaten to a jelly by the sticks of the guards. It doesn't pay. Me, I am resigned to destiny; I shall remain here one year, then walk out. My plans are made, and require only patience."

Jossas was a wizard with locks, keys, handcuffs. If sliding out of his irons would have done him the least good, he could have been free an hour after they were riveted on.

"If your plans are made," said Vidocq, "mine are not; so lend me a hand. My chief trouble is the leg-irons, which are riveted on for good."

Jossas grinned. "Lend you a hand? Why not? If you escape, or even make a good try, while I stay here, it'll suit my own plans excellently. I'll answer for your irons, if you can figure out the rest. It'll take time, however. I have false rivets, each in two parts which screw together, hidden away…. Where? None of your business. They'll not be found, since they've already escaped search. They were supplied to me before I got here, by a friend. I'll give you a couple, if you'll send me back two hundred francs after you make good your escape."

"Done," Vidocq said promptly. "But how shall I get rid of my present rivets?—which are not false, I assure you!"

"Leave that to me; it'll take six weeks of work at night, but I can do it."

Vidocq had already made his own plans, but he was not doing any talking about them, even to Jossas....

A month passed, and two months. By means of a tiny file, no larger than a toothpick, passed to Jossas from outside, the rivets in Vidocq's permanent leg-irons were removed and replaced by false rivets. This little operation required a full six weeks of patient and minute labor, at odd times of the night.

To obtain such a file was not extra difficult. There were plenty of people, even among the guards, willing to furnish such articles, at a price—and later squeal on the unhappy convict. There were others who would not squeal. Vidocq, learning all these things by degrees, made his own contacts.

T H E O N E alleviation of his miserable lot, was that the inmates were kept shaven. This was not for cleanliness, but to further recapture if any escaped. Further, all Toulon knew that a standing reward of fifty francs was offered for any information leading to the recapture of an escaped convict. All this lay at the outer end of the chain—after the escape was made.

Along the inner end, Vidocq perceived the utter impossibility of escaping from this hulk itself. If he could get himself released from the double irons and have his arms free, if he could get sent to daily labor among the less suspect convicts, then he would have a real chance for a break. He figured out exactly what that real chance would be, how it might be turned to advantage; then he put his mind on the problem of getting assigned to a labor gang.

Three months had passed; and Vidocq, even in the eyes of Father Mathieu, had proved himself an ideal prisoner.

Father Mathieu was an old, viciously cruel guard, in immediate charge of the group surrounding Vidocq. Despite age, he was one of those squarely hewn men who never wear out, his

face wrinkled
and hideous,
snuff always
on his lapel,
cudgel always
under his arm,
ready to beat
the nearest
convict at the
first excuse. He
knew by heart
every trick of
a convict; he
was said to
read their very
thoughts; and
perhaps there
was some truth
in this saying.

"You are
almost as low
as pigs," he
said to his
charges one
day. "Not quite,
but almost. You
are enemies of
society. A pig is
the most invet-
erate enemy of

The Prison Ship.

mankind. Just a little more, my honest fellows, and you would
be in the class of pigs."

A pig, the enemy of mankind? That was absurd. Father
Mathieu chuckled gleefully; he liked to propound odd queries,
start an argument, then take it as an excuse for a beating all

around. This time, however, he had a surprise, for Vidocq spoke up in agreement.

"Father Mathieu speaks the exact truth, boys. Anyone raised in the country knows that if a baby falls into a pigpen, the pigs will eat it. That proves the inborn and instinctive hatred of pigs for humanity in general."

Father Mathieu was so astonished that he almost beamed. His excuse for a beating was gone, but Vidocq had given an actual reason for his haphazard statement.

From this moment, Vidocq cultivated the friendship of Father Mathieu. As he never occasioned the least trouble, never went into a wild insane rage, and accepted his beatings without a curse in exchange, Father Mathieu came to tolerate him to a certain degree.

ONE NIGHT Vidocq nudged his companion in misery.

"It is farewell, my friend. Tomorrow I start on my way."

"Eh?" muttered Jossas in surprise. "Not really?"

"Really," Vidocq said calmly. "Have you been watching Antoine, that fellow who cut his wife's throat? Listen; you can hear him groaning now."

"Yes, that infected wound," said Jossas. "The surgeon was looking at him today. He'll probably get a trip to the infirmary about day after tomorrow."

"Precisely. When they work on him, I shall be there."

"So?" Jossas whistled thoughtfully. "I wish you luck, Vidocq. I don't know your plans, but all the same—"

"I have no plans," said Vidocq, not altogether truthfully. "Except for the first step or two. After that, things will take care of themselves."

"You are wise," the other rejoined after a moment. "Yes; you are wise. You are the sort of person who is adaptable to circumstances, who knows when not to hesitate. Ninety-nine out of a hundred here would lose their heads. You'll do the right thing, at the right instant."

"Such as not forgetting my promise to send back the two hundred francs I owe you," Vidocq murmured craftily.

Jossas laughed.

"Well said, and it proves my argument. I might gain fifty francs by betraying you, and I'd lose the two hundred. Correct, my friend. Luck attend you! If you need anything sent in to you—"

"I've arranged for everything to be sent to me at the infirmary tomorrow evening."

"The devil! You certainly have confidence. You'll have a job persuading that beast of a surgeon there's anything wrong with you."

Vidocq chuckled softly. "He's not the man to persuade. He takes the word of Father Mathieu, if you've noticed."

At this, Jossas laughed again, with amused admiration.

WHEN FATHER Mathieu came on duty next morning, Vidocq lay in his chains, his food untouched, his eyes open.

"Hello!" Father Mathieu walked over and spoke to Jossas. "What's the matter with him?"

Jossas shrugged. "I don't know. He talks queerly."

"Shamming, eh?" Father Mathieu brought his cudgel into play, but Vidocq merely looked up and made a gesture with his right hand. The guard stooped. The words of Vidocq were uncouth and harsh, difficult to distinguish.

"Something wrong. Hard—hard to talk. Can't use left—leg or hand. What is it?"

Father Mathieu straightened up.

"Can't use your left leg, eh?" His stick came down with a thud on the leg of Vidocq, and again on his outstretched left arm. "Feel that?"

"No," muttered Vidocq. "Something wrong. Poisoned, perhaps—"

The stick came down again. Father Mathieu jerked out a knife and prodded Vidocq's left leg. Then his right. At this last,

Vidocq uttered a piercing cry and moved his right leg convulsively. Father Mathieu straightened up.

"Poisoned? Not much. You go to the infirmary, my lad; I've seen this before now," he stated. "A seizure, that's what it is. Paralysis. A stroke. Never fear, you'll get over it in a few days and be back at our little tavern; it's only the first one."

An hour later Vidocq's wrists were freed of their irons, he was unlocked from the wall shackles, and was carried ashore to the infirmary. The surgeon had made only a brief examination. Here in the filth and squalor of the prison hulk, he was content to take the word of Father Mathieu.

As they carried him out, Vidocq fluttered an eyelid at Jossas; but so well did he play his part, that it was the right eye with which he winked.

The infirmary, by contrast, was paradise. When Vidocq had been bathed, his prison blouse and trousers were replaced and he was left on a cot; his leg-irons, permanently riveted in place, were assurance that he could not escape ever if sound and well. Besides, there was a guard posted at the outer door.

This infirmary was merely a room of some size. Outside it was the office and the room where the surgeon and his assistant, who was a nurse-of-all-work, performed any needed operations.

In this paradise Vidocq lay the rest of the day. Two other convicts were here, tied down to their cots; they had fever, and their babble filled the air.

As might be anticipated, the infirmary arrangements were crude in the extreme. There was no fear of any escape from here, for the guarded walls and yards of the arsenal lay outside. It was from here, however, that Vidocq had planned to escape.

All that day and evening he played his part to perfection. The surgeon, assistant and the guard chatted. Servants came in. Officials stepped in for a pipe and a drink with the surgeon. Talking went on freely. The assistant even talked as he fed broth to the helpless Vidocq. A new prison commissioner had been appointed and would arrive in a day or so.

Most exciting news was that the frigate *Meuron* lay at anchor
close by—due for extensive repairs, having been battered by an
English frigate. Her master carpenter and half a dozen more
of her men were being brought into the infirmary this same
evening, and the place would be filled.

"What about that fellow from the prison hulk, with the old
wound?" demanded the assistant.

"Oh," said the surgeon, "go aboard and fix him up there. A
convict doesn't matter; we can't bother about him, when we have
honest seamen to fill the beds here."

IN A flash, Vidocq's entire plan of escape was all washed up.

He had not, as a matter of fact, arranged to have anything sent
him here; he had lied on that point to Jossas. Instead, he had
hinged everything on the wound of the man Antoine. While
the surgeon and assistant were working on the man in the oper-
ating-room, Vidocq had intended to slip his irons, take their
garments from the office, and calmly walk out of the place.

No go now. And a new commissioner was coming, would be
making inspection visits....

That same night, the master carpenter and others of the
Meuron's crew filled the infirmary. Even before they arrived,
Vidocq had made contact with a servant cleaning up the place;
he arranged with the woman for what he wanted, promising
payment later. Such a promise was nearly always kept; it was
a good gamble. An escaped convict invariably paid such debts.
All that Vidocq demanded was a curled wig, a seaman's shirt,
and a seaman's cap.

These reached him the next evening and were put under his
mattress.

Another two days, and his response to the surgeon's treatment
was gratifying. He was obviously recovering from his stroke.
And when, next afternoon, the place was tidied up for inspection by the commissioner, Vidocq had recovered his powers of
speech.

The new official, a petty politician, was a pursy, solemn person,

Vidocq nudged his companion. "It is farewell,
my friend. Tomorrow I start on my way."

very earnest in his new position. As he came past, Vidocq made
a piteous gesture and begged to be allowed to speak to him.

"Why, of course!" exclaimed the worthy man. "You have some
complaint? Make it! I shall do you justice, my word upon it!"

Vidocq, who had appraised his man at a glance, burst into
tears.

"Good sir, I beg you in the name of common humanity not

to leave me among the wretches on the prison hulk! Load me with chains, place me in a dungeon, set me at the hardest kind of labor—anything but a return to that place! You can have no conception of what it means to be among those men. They are brutes, rather than men, of the lowest type, boasting of their past crimes and excesses, looking forward to new ones when free. I am not guiltless, it is true; I deserve all that the law has given me. Still, I am a man; I have hopes of expiating my misdeeds and regaining my rightful place in society, when the time comes. It is not indulgence that I crave; it is salvation from that sink of infamy!"

He paused, for he was out of breath. The commissioner was obviously touched by this sort of appeal, and turned to the surgeon.

"Is it true? Are they so bad?"

"Worse," said the surgeon dryly; "and this fellow is one of the worst. Still, he has a good record; he's made no trouble, I understand."

"The vilest of men may hope for redemption," Vidocq said humbly. "I ask for nothing except a chance to prove myself worthy. Chains? Load me with fetters! Punishment, as you please. Work, the hardest sort of labor—"

Again the commissioner turned to the surgeon.

"When will this fellow be able to work?"

"In a couple of days, at his present rate of progress."

"Then have him placed on the timber gang in the shipyards adjoining."

Vidocq sobbed out his thanks. The gratified, pompous, worthy commissioner passed on.

DURING THE next two days, Vidocq astonished the surgeon, who was a rough and ready practitioner, by his consistent recovery. His recovery was certified; with morning he would go to the timber gang of some fifty convicts.

Long before the dawn, he wakened, stripped, and donned the

shirt or jersey that marked him for a seaman. The wool cap and the wig he tucked under his belt. Over all, he drew the flaming red blouse that marked him for a convict, and satisfied himself that it quite concealed the jersey. Then he went back to sleep.

His plans had now reached their end. From this time on, he depended wholly on chance and his own ability to take advantage of it.

The guards came for him early; a bowl of thin soup, and he was off,

"It is not indulgence that I crave; it is salvation from that sink of infamy."

chewing a crust of bread as he marched between his guards. He was taken straight to the basin where the battered frigate lay warped to the dock, and was turned over to the chain-gang that had just begun work.

VIDOCQ'S SHARP eyes took in everything. Up the harbor lay Toulon—city docks and streets that offered, as he thought, complete freedom. Here were the busy arsenal and dock-yards, dotted scarlet with the red shirts of convicts, heav-

ily sprinkled with the shirts and wool caps of seamen likewise
at work, but free to come and go.

Recommended for easy labor until fully recovered from his
stroke, Vidocq was told off with a puny, knavish Gascon to clear
a huge pile of débris—old boards and lumber stacked high—
which remained a hundred feet from the wharf at which lay the
Menron. The foreman snapped at them to get at the job, and they
moved off, dragging their leg-irons.

"I've heard of you, Vidocq," said the Gascon. "They tell me
you're a sly one, that you've boasted you were going to make a
break."

"That was true, before I was ill," said Vidocq, shaking his head
sadly. "But not now, comrade. It'll be a long time before I can
think of escape."

In a flash it came to him that he must act now, at once; this
Gascon was all set to catch him tripping and tip off the foreman. If he waited until the work-gangs knew his face, until he
was well known to these convicts, it would be more difficult.
And there was the master carpenter from the frigate, now in
the infirmary.

"You tackle it from this side," he said to the Gascon, as they
came to the huge pile. "I'll clear out the light stuff from the other
side. Then we can move the heavier pieces together."

A ring of authority in his voice precluded any objection. He
slipped around to the other side of the pile; a glance showed him
no one close at hand. He stooped, loosened the false rivets, and
was out of his leg-irons. Shoving them in among the lumber,
he whipped off his flaming red shirt and shoved it after. He
clapped the wig on his head, pulled the wool cap over it and his
forehead, and struck away.

"The right thing at the right instant," Jossas had said.

At this particular instant one misstep would have ruined
him—literally. Vidocq did not make it. Instead of showing
the hesitant, leg-dragging step of the convict, he stepped out
briskly, nimbly, straight for the wharf. The curly black hair, the

"Suppose," said Vidocq, "you were talking with the very men who had just escaped!"

seaman's jersey, attracted no casual glance. Other seamen were going to and fro, sturdy barefooted men with pantaloons rolled up, like his own.

Once on the frigate's deck, he boldly approached an officer and asked for the master carpenter.

"I was told to report to him here, sir," he added.

"He's not here. His mate is forward; report to him."

Vidocq marched forward. Before he knew it, he found himself

among a large group of convicts at work here, putting supplies into one of the frigate's barges. Panic struck him; these were men he knew. On the way to Toulon he had become acquainted with them all. They could not fail to recognize him.

Like a flash, he turned aside to the gangway, and fell in among a file of seamen going down to the barge.

Once there, he took place beside another man at a huge sweep. Here, once again, a single wrong action would have meant disaster; he had never been at sea in his life. But he watched the other men narrowly. As the barge shoved out, he imitated their actions and handled his oar passably well.

His heart leaped when he saw that the barge was heading toward the city. He put his weight on the oar, like the others. Inwardly he was tense, alert, watchful of everything. His oar-mate spoke to him in a Breton accent; he responded in the patois of Auvergne, scarcely intelligible to the other man. The barge drew on and on; the arsenal and hulks and dockyard fell away. They headed in toward the city wharves.

"Get this lading ashore, and you have an hour's leave," said the officer in charge. "Any man who's not back at the boat in an hour, gets a flogging. See to it!"

A flogging! Vidocq chuckled to himself. Little he cared for such things now! Once ashore, once in the town, he was free; all care was behind him. Before that hour was up, he would be past the gates and legging it out into the open country, for the north and Paris!

The barge was lined up, the cargo was unloaded. Vidocq worked like a Trojan; it was the price of freedom.

Suddenly a new fear seized him, and sent the sweat down his face in rivulets. Unless he reached the gates and got clear before his escape was discovered, he might yet be a lost man. When the alarm guns signified an escape, Toulon was searched to its very dregs. With strained senses, he worked on.

The task was finished, the seamen dismissed. Instantly Vidocq was gone. He headed straight for the nearest exit from the town—the Italian gate, it was then termed, Toulon being walled and fortified. With each moment, with each step, he dreaded hearing the alarm signal; it would make each man scan his neighbor.

THE GATE at last! About it a throng of peasants, some entering, some leaving. Vidocq, now in an agony of suspense, edged his way among the file going out. Suddenly he caught his breath, as he noticed that those ahead of him handed the guards a slip of green cardboard in passing.

His heart chilled. In reply to some jocular question, the guard officer laughingly said:

"Anyone without a green ticket would have a hard time leaving Toulon, let me tell you! We have too many convicts and deserters trying to slip away, to take any chances."

Somehow, Vidocq edged out of the throng again. A green ticket, eh? Devil take it, he had known nothing about this contingency. Probably it was some new regulation. And how to get around it, with every wasted moment bringing peril, he could not tell.

He wandered blindly, aimlessly along the street. For once, he was at wit's end; this sudden shattering of his plan had left him unable to think. He halted before a shop window and was staring at it with unseeing eyes, when a voice startled him.

"Hello there, sailor-man! Looking for company?"

He turned. A young woman was smiling at him, a not unattractive young woman. Her profession was at once evident to him. Vidocq shook his head, with a grimace.

"Sorry, my dear, but I haven't a sou."

At this instant came the sound he had been dreading with all his soul—the three cannon-shots. The girl clapped her hands suddenly.

"Good! Good!" she exclaimed with an air of satisfaction. "An escape!"

"What's that to you?" Vidocq demanded sourly. "Fifty francs if you catch the poor devil, eh?"

She turned on him with an angry flash of the eyes. "How little you know me! I'm poor enough, but I'd never touch that sort of money. Poor men! They're to be pitied. If I could only save them all, I would. I've saved two or three already."

"Suppose," said Vidocq, "you were talking with the very man who had just escaped. Suppose he was unable to get out of town without a green ticket—"

"Bah! I'd help him gladly," said the girl. "Why, if it were this very moment, as you say, I'd show him how to get out of the city in another five minutes!"

Vidocq stared at her. Every reasoning instinct told him that such a woman, despite her words, would leap at the reward. And yet—five minutes?

"Very well," he said quietly, and pulled off his cap and wig for an instant to prove his words. "I'm the man who has just escaped. Now help me—for if you don't, I can't leave the city."

The right thing, at the right instant! As she stared, he doubted this, cursed his own impulsive action. One cry from her would have him seized. The reward would be hers.

"I thought you were," she said, "from the way you just now spoke! Very well, my friend; you doubt me, you suspect me. I see it in your eyes. You're wrong. And to prove it, there's your way of escape. Quickly! The cemetery is outside the walls."

She pointed to a funeral procession coming up the street, with people uncovering respectfully as it passed.

VIDOCQ COMPREHENDED instantly; he seized her hand, gave it one grateful pressure, and was gone into the throngs about the gates.

The funeral, like all such affairs in France, was a solemn business. Behind the crawling hearse with its nodding black plumes followed the immediate family in a little knot—on foot, of course. Behind these, again, came a long line of friends and relatives. Among these were a number of seamen. A navy funeral in Toulon was a common occurrence.

When the procession reached the gates and crowded up at the momentary halt, Vidocq edged in among the mourners. Then on again, trudging along the dusty way, while the guards uncovered in respect to the dead. No one thought of demanding the green tickets from these mourners, who were obviously coming back into the city so soon.

Two minutes later Vidocq was out of Toulon; but the talk, all around him, was of the signal just heard, and the escaped convict, and the reward. The dead man was forgotten. To make off was now impossible, and Vidocq followed on to the cemetery.

There he fell into lamentations with the others, saw the body disposed, and advanced in turn to the edge of the grave, casting a handful of earth on the coffin. Only then did he manage to withdraw among the tombstones, carefully lose himself, and finally take to his heels.

He was free.

NO SILENCE fell in the prison cell to denote the story's end; but Manning's hands drooped motionless, and he smiled at his wide-eyed friend. And Cotterel said, with a deep, sharp breath:

"That's all?"

"That's all," said Manning's fluttering fingers. "Isn't it enough?"

"I think it is," Cotterel answered reflectively. "Yes, I see what you mean, all right; the instinct to do the right thing at the right time, sure. If he hadn't made up his mind on the spot to trust that girl, he might have been in a jam."

"Not instinct, but sharp wits," Manning corrected him. "A cool, balanced brain all the way. Some men call it instinct, but it's not. You have just that sort of a brain, but you've let it get a bit out of control. Now, get it in hand once more!"

"I'll do it!" Cotterel leaned forward, his eyes shining, his face alight. "Manning, with your knowledge about such things, with your skill, with your foresight, we can make the break where anyone else would fail! You weren't speaking lightly? You're in earnest about it?"

"I promised I'd help you escape from these walls,"—and if ever a man's fingers could achieve solemn speech, Manning's did then—"and I'll keep that promise."

"Shake!" said Cotterel, and the two men gripped hands.

THE CHRISTIAN SLAVE

THIS SIXTH OF THESE SAGAS OF STRANGE ESCAPE DEALS WITH
AN ENGLISHMAN HELD CAPTIVE BY THE MOORS, AND WITH THE
UNFORESEEN POSSIBILITY THAT CHANGED THE WORLD FOR HIM.

FOR DAYS, now, Cotterel had been glooming in the cell, the shop, the yard, scarcely speaking, regarding all around him with eyes of sullen suspicion. At last Manning, his cellmate, ventured a kindly inquiry.

"Leave me alone!" Cotterel burst out. "Keep to yourself. Keep your nose out of my affairs. I'm through with you, understand? I'm applying to the Warden tomorrow to change my cell, and that settles it. I'm tired of your eternal advice."

Old Manning, in for life like Cotterel, regarded the younger man with no responding heat in his wise, gentle eyes.

This was the first savage break in their friendship. In all these months, they had occupied the same cell; repeatedly had Manning, in his shrewd knowledge of prison life, intervened to save Cotterel from impulsive folly.

Now he recognized the symptoms. Old Manning knew this to be the softest stir in the country; but behind the velvet glove was a hand of iron. He himself was deserving of all he got. Cotterel, on the other hand, was in for a crime he had not committed; Manning felt this to be true, and sympathized. He could understand Cotterel's wild beating at the bars. But— change cells, end their friendship? This was different.

He studied the haggard features, the desperate eyes, the clenched lips, of Cotterel. Between the two had grown up a strong and real friendship. Manning liked his companion rarely; himself a lonely old man, an artist who had gone wrong, he had given himself without stint to Cotterel, and until now had been repaid in kind. Yet, even now, he saw that this surly, suspicious, snapping mood had something else behind it and was not natural. Prison-wise as he was, knowing Cotterel and others in this

hell on earth, he could guess at the truth.

"So," he said in his silent, deft way, "you're figuring on a break again."

"None of your business," snapped Cotterel. "Why in hell don't you keep to yourself? I'm done with you and your blasted smooth talk. Every time something turns up, you argue me out of it. Suds Jackson got away two weeks ago. I'd have been with him now if you hadn't stuck your oar in. Shut up! To hell with you!"

Manning ignored the savage glare, the acid words. His affection for the younger man was too precious a thing to be so dismissed. This was not the first time Cotterel had been close to the lunatic fringe.

"If Suds Jackson could do it, you can do it, eh?" he observed.

"Shut up!" blurted Cotterel angrily.

Manning persisted. At the moment, there was no bar to their talking. There was no bar at any time, for that matter. Old Manning had not uttered a word aloud for years. He was dumb.

His fingers spoke for him. Those deft, nimble fingers, so

apt at sketching or engraving, had put him behind the bars. During the months of companionship, Cotterel had learned the finger-talk. He did not have to use it himself unless he liked, for Manning was not deaf; but it gave them relief from the rule of silence that was clamped down now and again.

"Suppose Suds Jackson had been shot making the break?" he said. "And you with him?"

"Better be shot than here for life," rejoined Cotterel.

Ah! This was better. At least the ice was broken, Cotterel was willing to talk. Manning's fingers flew again, and the sullen gaze of Cotterel was not averted.

"A curious thing," Manning went on calmly. "Very curious. There's a possibility that certainly has never occurred to Suds Jackson, and it has never occurred to you; it never would occur—"

"I'm not interested," broke in Cotterel. "Lay off, I tell you! To hell with you and your possibilities. I know 'em all."

"Not this one; yet it's perhaps the greatest and most powerful of all. The possibility unseen and invisible, the one thing that you wouldn't think of, Cotterel. I'm not interfering with anything you want to do. I agree that death would be a blessed release from this place; I'd take a bullet myself for one day of freedom, just like Forbes. And yet you can't afford to neglect the one thing he neglected, the one possibility that's never foreseen, the thought that never occurred to him."

COTTEREL LIFTED sultry eyes. "I'm neglecting nothing. If you've got anything to say, spit it out and get it over. You're not going to argue me out of what I mean to do. Who's Forbes?"

Manning smiled, a whimsical touch in his face.

"Argue? Not a bit of it. I merely want to give you every possible weapon, make sure you neglect nothing. And this is something you've certainly neglected. Suds Jackson neglected it."

Cotterel scowled. "What are you talking about? Suds Jackson got clear. And if it wasn't for you, I'd be with him right now. Free!"

Manning nodded. More sensitive than most, the prison grapevine brought him odd bits of information that others missed. Only this afternoon, he had heard something, and he was expecting momentary confirmation. At least, it would serve him now as a basis on which to cast the dice. For he must gamble, if he were to save Cotterel—and himself.

He did not blink the fact that he had a selfish interest in this friendship. It made this prison life at least endurable, gave him something rare and precious for which to live and exist. It was very close now to being broken asunder in Cotterel's desperate agony of soul.

"Don't be like Forbes," he said. Cotterel snarled an oath.

"And who's Forbes?"

"Archibald Forbes. A Scot, a young fellow like you. If you want me to tell you what's in my mind, you must let me do it my own way, Cotterel. I can't make you see the importance of this unseen possibility, unless you agree. And it's vitally important to you, if you aim to get away."

Cotterel gave him a sulky stare.

"All right. I know there's a catch in it, but go ahead. It won't have any effect. I'm bound to get out, and I'm certain about everything, and I don't give a damn if I do get a bullet."

Manning laughed, in his silent way.

"That sounds like Forbes. He was a prisoner in Meknes, the capital of Morocco, when that country was a real empire, at the close of the seventeenth century. The emperor, Ismail, was probably the most despotic monarch the world ever knew. He set up the doctrine that Morocco and everything and everyone in it was all his absolute personal property. He got away with it."

"Why?" demanded Cotterel as the other paused.

Manning gave no sign that this indication of interest delighted his heart.

"Because he was both cruel and smart. So cruel, that everyone stood in deathly fear of him; it was calculated that in the course of his life he had killed twenty-five thousand people with his own hand. So smart, nobody could outwit him. And personally so brave and able that none of his bravest men, singly or in crowds, could stand against him with any weapon. He was a phenomenon."

"SOUNDS LIKE it," grunted Cotterel. "Wasn't he the guy who had a lot of Christian slaves?"

"About thirty thousand—and Forbes was one of them. Ismail used those slaves, and his own people as well, to build the immense walls of Meknes; incredible walls, defenses, palaces. He had fifty palaces, five hundred wives, and around a thousand sons—the daughters were strangled at birth. However, let's stick to Forbes.

"He was a Scots seaman, taken aboard some ship the Sallee Rovers brought in, and like all other Christian captives, was sent as a slave to Meknes. We know every detail of his story, of his marvelous escape. Ismail never freed any slaves until they were too worn out for further work; then he'd let the Redemptionist Fathers ransom them. These fathers were allowed to live in Meknes, and gave their lives to the redemption of Christian captives from among the Moors. They've left us the story of Forbes.

"He was one of those wiry men, not bulging with muscle,

but of superhuman ability to endure. Such men accomplish the impossible."

Manning paused; then his flying fingers went on with the astonishing story of Forbes, enclosed in such a prison as the world has seldom known—a prison, such as Russia or Germany today affords, in which the prison consists of the entire country.

FORBES WAS intelligent, shrewd, able. He spent a couple of years in this living hell, before reaching the point where he chose death rather than more of it; he must escape or go under, and death would be welcome release. For a time he worked around the menagerie maintained by the Emperor Ismail. The palace grounds, surrounded by a triple wall, were of incredible size—the stable alone contained a thousand horses. Ismail had a huge menagerie, and did not hesitate to fight with the wild beasts himself. He thought nothing of throwing a slave to the lions, or a soldier, or one of his courtiers. One day he threw Forbes to them, but the lions knew him and left him alone. So Ismail put him on the hard-labor gang, the building gang. And with this, Forbes knew he was a goner, and determined to escape or die.

The daily life facing him was beyond description; that any man could survive under such conditions was past belief. Yet a standing force of some thirty thousand Christians, and as many Berbers and Arabs, was maintained. The slave quarters in Meknes consisted of vast chambers, partly underground, where the slaves were huddled like wild beasts in filth and rags, after it was too dark to work. Here they were herded by a regular night guard, a burly Andalusian Moor, who beat or tortured them at will. With earliest dawn, they were again taken out in stumbling hordes to the labor.

The building operations, of which Ismail himself was architect and chief overseer, were simple. The enormous, massive walls ran for uncounted miles. They consisted of a mastic, a mixture of sand with limestone and gravel, pounded down between forms of timber. When a slave was killed or died, he was pounded into the walls with the mastic. The walls of Meknes today are filled with Christian bones....

The food was starvation diet. The work was severe. Berbers and Arabs, criminals or rebellious subjects, were mingled with the Christians, for Ismail, himself a black, ruled with black Sudanese soldiers and ground down the Arabs beyond any rebellion. His was a throne of blood, ruled with sharp steel.

At all times the labor was pressed, but especially when Ismail appeared. If it did not go to his liking, he used sword and spear in a passionate frenzy; he was mad with the desire to build more walls. He cut down slave, soldier, noble or prime minister alike. In more humane moments, his chief feat of prowess was to mount his horse, and in the same flowing motion behead the man who held his stirrup; he was equally capable of fighting an enraged lion, armed only with his sword.

He prodded the hapless slaves to superhuman exertions. They died like flies; more came in every day to replace them, from ships captured by the Barbary rovers. Spanish, English, French, Italian—all nations mingled here in a hell of sweating death.

Forbes resolved to escape.

His red hair and blue eyes were not against him; Morocco was full of Berbers with similar complexions. He was hard as nails, emaciated, hairy, powerful. Soon he would lose strength and courage and hope, like some of them who had been here twenty and thirty years; now was the time, if ever. He spoke Arabic with moderate fluency.

Escape by day was simply unthinkable; evasion by night was the only way, but escape was utterly impossible. He knew it well enough. Many a man had tried. Here were two Spaniards who had tried, hard, vigorous men; now they labored in chains, after having been beaten and tortured out of human semblance.

Forbes weighed the chances coolly. With luck, he might do it. Without, not.

The night guard, the jail doors—the first step. Once out of this prison, he would be in the city, in Meknes, gates closed and

walls patrolled. Once out of Meknes, he would have the olive
orchards of the valley—and beyond those, desert and mountain. To reach the seacoast, across those leagues of stony desert
and savage mountain, where he would be hunted day and night,
where every man's hand would be against him with fanatic reli-
gious hatred, where he could find no food and little water, was
an appalling gamble.

And when he reached the sea-coast, he would find only
Moors. Ismail had driven all the Christian powers out of
Morocco; the Spaniards alone held footing at Ceuta. Their
other places had fallen. The Portuguese had been driven out.
The English had been driven out of Tangier. Ismail, all but
supreme in conquest of the Christian, had decreed that Morocco
should wear only yellow slippers henceforth, as a token of rejoic-
ing. They are still universally worn today, though the reason is
forgotten by the wearers.

THAT THE obstacles were insuperable, Forbes knew; he
accepted them. There was only one thing he did not anticipate—
the one thing no prisoner thinks about when contemplating
escape. This one thing never occurred to him.

It never occurs to anyone, until too late. What was it? Wait!

In this land of blood, where death was at one's elbow day and
night, where heads were piled by the thousand in the market-
place after every campaign, Forbes was well aware that except by
spilling blood, he could not escape. In fact, he had a few scores
he was only too anxious to pay off in Moorish blood.

He had watched the emperor closely. He knew Ismail was no
madman, as some called him, but a very deep and crafty fellow,
aiming to hold by fear a throne that had destroyed its occupants
hitherto very quickly. And from this, Forbes got his prime idea.
Others had tried to escape by stealth, by hiding, by slippery
evasion. He would eschew all these things.

In this land of blood, he would do what no one else had
done—escape by blood. So, having weighed every detail, Forbes

awaited his chance. It was the rainy season, and he wanted a night of rain....

It came. A thin, fine drizzle of rain, when Moors were huddled to the very eyes in the hoods of their jellabs. Ismail had come out to speed the work that day; he had killed two overseers, had ordered a chief overseer drawn through the city at the tail of a horse and then impaled, and had ordered that

"Well, dog? Tell me the plot quickly.... What is their plan?"

a double portion of work be finished on the morrow. The prison was filled with groans and lamentations; the morrow would see wretched backs red with whip-strokes.

Forbes slept. A little past midnight, he wakened. The burly Andalusian, jingling his bunch of keys, was passing among the huddled sleepers, amusing himself by kicking one and another. Forbes beckoned him, and he came, grinning.

"Well, dog of an Englishman! What is it?"

"Quiet!" murmured Forbes, with a cautious look around. "If I tell you of a plot to escape, is there a reward?"

"Aye, by Allah!" The other grinned again. "Who?"

"I can't tell you here. They'd kill me! Take me outside with you."

The Andalusian launched a kick at him, and emitted a roar.

"Up, dog, up! Come with me. I have a pleasant little task for you—it's time the latrines were cleaned. Come on, come on!"

With a simulated groan, Forbes rose and followed. The Andalusian had his home in a room at the prison gate, where he could call guards if necessary. They were seldom needed, so broken and worn in body and spirit were these slaves.

IN THIS hovel of his own, where a lamp burned dimly, the Andalusian turned. Forbes had seen into this room twice a day, morning and evening; he knew everything in it, knew exactly what he would do on this occasion. He came in and closed the door.

"Well, dog? Tell me the plot, quickly. Who is in it?"

"The three Spaniards who came last week," said Forbes, crossing to the farther wall where a stout bar of oak leaned in a corner.

"By Allah and Allah!" exclaimed the keeper. "What is their plan?"

The only reply of Forbes was to catch up the oak bar, whirl it, and strike. The blow cut short the alarm-shout of the Andalusian; and the burly man collapsed, with his skull shattered.

Forbes listened; the closed door, the rain, had silenced the cry. There was no alarm. Now, unhurriedly he went about his business.

FIRST, HE ate. Food was here, and water; he filled himself for the first time in over two years. Cold *couscous*, dates, bread, he made into small packets and laid aside. He hacked off his long, matted hair and shaved his skull, Moorish fashion, leaving only the one lock of hair by which the angel would presumably carry him to Paradise. He trimmed his beard roughly, and then dressed himself in what clothes he could find here—baggy linen

"Out of the way!" snarled the Moor. His whip slashed.
Forbes laughed—laughed as his knife flashed.

trousers, a dirty white robe, and over all an old brown jellab. On his horny naked feet he put the yellow slippers of the keeper.

Around his neck he slung the long curved knife taken from the dead man. He found a little money, a few coins of copper and silver, which he took gladly. Then, aware that earliest dawn would find him the object of a frenzied and determined search, he took the keys, opened the main doors, and slipped out into the street. The drizzle of rain kept any guards close. Hood pulled over head, he shuffled along the streets of pounded earth, until he found the place he sought—a dim light coming from behind screens, at a doorway that was never closed.

This was the Grand Mesjid, or Mosque as the French called

it, on the market square. No Christian had ever been inside it, but Forbes had picked up bountiful knowledge.

He turned in at the entrance. The doorkeeper was snoring blissfully; leaving his slippers, now mud-splashed past recognition, beside the sleeper, Forbes made for the courtyard of ablutions. Here he was alone, with a dim-burning lamp. Stripping, he enjoyed the luxury of a thorough wash at the huge basin of living water. This was not only a luxury, but a necessity. The slave-odor was an identifying thing, stronger even than the stench which clung to the open-sewage streets of every Arab town. Once rid of this odor—and at no other time of the day or night could he have thus rid himself of it—he could breathe more easily, both literally and figuratively.

Veiled once more in his damp jellab, he turned his steps toward the interior of the mosque. Here, upon a corner of one of the great carpets, he sank down with a sigh of relief, freed himself of the jellab, and made a number of prostrations toward the *mihrab*, the niche that faced toward Mecca, in the Moslem manner; it was merely a precaution in case he had attracted any attention.

This vast interior was not empty. Lamps lit the gorgeous tiles of the walls, the curious Arabic inscriptions, the lacy carved and painted plaster-work, the carved and painted beams, the screens here and there. Dim figures were sprawled here and there, some in slumber, others in meditation. A furiously dirty holy man from some marabout outside the city, naked except for loin-cloth and shaggy hair, leaned against a pillar and mechanically murmured Koranic verses. Occasional snores sounded.

As Forbes knew, to these people a mosque was more than a place to which men came for prayer at the appointed hours. It was a place for gossip and meeting, for meditation, for rest and study and enjoyment of beauty; it was an escape from the world of blood and death around. For him, it was safety.

No one would dream of looking for him here—where, if discovered, he would be torn to shreds by the hands of enraged fanatics. He needed no jellab to hide him; his shaven skull with its top-knot was the mark of a Moslem, and no one would give him even a passing second glance. That naked holy man by the pillar had the shaggy red hair of a Berber, even redder than Forbes' own.

Leaning against the wall, Forbes slept.

A CLAMOR of voices startled him wide awake; someone in passing gave him a kick, a friendly admonition. It was the moment of early morning prayer; the quavering voice of the blind muezzin came faintly from the high minaret above, though flags frequently took the place of muezzins, in Morocco. Men were trooping in all around.

Forbes did not know the prayers; he did not need to know them, so long as there was no suspicion aroused. He prostrated himself as the others did; he moved his lips as he rose from each bow, and amid the babel of voices his own was not missed. Someone, during the night, had left a rosary of black beads in the corner near-by. Forbes appropriated it, leaned back against the wall, dropped his beard on his breast and closed his eyes, and sat fingering the rosary in presumed meditation like many another.

Even now, he knew, the search was on. Gossip around him confirmed this.

"El Andalous with his head bashed in—by Allah, a blow! The Christian dog got away, but they'll find him. The city is being searched. He's hiding in the palace grounds, they say."

The hours passed. As each prayer-hour came, Forbes went through the ritual; it was beginning to get on his nerves, but he squelched down the gusty fear and forced himself to it. All around, men came in, talked business, ate, gossiped, prayed. Forbes ate, also; he listened, slept, clutched the rosary ostentatiously, gave himself up to delicious rest.

THE LONG day droned through its length. At last came the prayer of sunset; as the crowd flooded out, Forbes mingled with it, hood over head. He got his mud-splashed slippers at the entrance and passed out into the street.

Shuffling along the narrow, twisting ways, he stopped at a baker's booth, bought more bread, stopped at another booth and bought dried dates. He was near the Mellah now, the quarter of the Jews, the ghetto near the gates; another mosque was here, and he entered it boldly enough.

All night he remained here, and in the morning, after the sunrise prayer, took up anew his challenge to destiny. Thus far, his scheme had succeeded admirably; now to leave the city.

Here he had picked his time, and his place, very shrewdly. Outside these walls was the animal market, where for a swarming mile the yellow ground was thronged with asses, horses, camels, with buyers from the city, with country-folk and lean Berbers from the hills. Further, it was Friday, the one day when all the native women poured forth to the cemeteries on the hillsides.

Forbes had reckoned aright, and joined the throng seeking egress. The day was fair and sunny; already the dust rose in thick shimmering clouds. The stalwart black Sudanese troops of Ismail, the blacks whom he bred like animals and educated from earliest youth to savage soldiering, paid little heed as the gabbling crowds flowed past. Behind him, Forbes beheld the high massive towers and walls fall away. He was free!

The fact gave him no elation; he was tensed to meet the perils ahead. He still had a little money left, and food was now the first thing to settle. First food, then transport.

HE MADE his way along the dusty lanes of the animal market, unhurried, stopping now and again to buy more food and eat it, or stow it safely away. Action was drawing close upon him, as he knew well; when the moment came, he must strike hard and without mercy, but he must choose the moment aright or lose everything.

The heat of the day came on, and found him a little way out of the throngs and dust, resting beneath an olive tree, watching with hawk gaze the yellowish highway that wound away from the city and the market through the olive valleys. Into Meknes

The Sicilian ran in, with drawn sword.
Out of the dust and blood rose Forbes,
hurling his pistol into the dark face.

poured the endless groups of wagons and animals bearing building materials, levied from all parts of the empire; bands of slaves
trudging along, parties of soldiers. Country-folk eased away
from the markets of the city.

Presently, in the hot lull of noon, Forbes saw that his moment
was come. To his left, the road dipped, beyond sight of the
animal market; that was why he had chosen this spot. Coming
from the market to his right, heaped high on the rump of his
ass in the native style, was a man. A man of some importance,

to judge from his snowy robes; no doubt some town gentleman going out to his country estate or his olive orchard.

Forbes rose and strode on down into the dip, and waited. The proud Moor came along on the sturdily trotting little animal, and Forbes turned with a whine.

"Alms, *sidi!* Alms, in the name of Allah!"

"Go ask of Allah, for he's richer than I am," snarled the Moor. "Out of the way!"

His whip slashed down, across the face of Forbes. And Forbes laughed—laughed as he sprang, as his knife flashed, as the Moor died.

Tugging the body aside among the trees, he stripped it, found money and took that, came back to the ass, and mounted. Sitting a-crupper like the natives, clad now in the snow-white jellab of fine wool, he pulled the hood about his head to keep out the sun, and fled.

Another barrier was past. There remained the leagues of desert, the snowy Atlas mountains, the sea-coast beyond.

Mile after mile the little animal put behind at its speedy trot. The sun was at the horizon when Forbes, heading his makeshift mount down into a steep gully, still following the dusty track of the road perforce, came slap upon a dozen of Ismail's black soldiers, horsemen, escorting a wagon laden with tribute grain.

He scuttled past with a muttered greeting. Forbes knew very well that he could not hope to pass for a native at close quarters, though his knowledge of the language was enough to serve in a pinch. He saw the eyes of the blacks roll enviously as he passed. This sleek ass, though nearly worthless in the open country, was a valuable piece of property in the city, and the soldiers were heading for Meknes.

One of them turned his horse, with a laugh, and struck back down the gully.

FORBES HEARD the horseman following him as he reached the trickling stream at the bottom; he heard the order to halt, and obeyed it. Dismounting, he stood silent as the horseman reined in, with a flood of negroid Arabic. Forbes could not understand the words at all, but he understood that this black was taking the ass; these swaggering Sudanese took what they liked from any Arab, and Ismail stood behind them.

Not dreaming of any resistance from this townsman, the soldier leaned far over in the saddle to catch the reins of the ass. As he leaned, the curved knife of Forbes flashed in the sunset, and flashed again, more redly. With a choked cry, the black pitched out of the saddle headlong.

Forbes caught the horse, swung up into the high saddle, and rode away at speed, nor slackened pace until the dusk of evening closed around him. A wild exultation filled his heart. Now he had everything—a good horse, a water-bottle, dried dates in plenty, and the stars to guide him!

During two days he kept on his way, avoiding the scattered villages, drifting ever toward the mountains and the coast. On the second day he ran into a party of Arabs, hunting. There was no evading them, so he rode among them boldly.

A renegade, said he, going an errand for the emperor. The lie got him through.

There were hundreds of renegades—poor devils who had changed their faith to save themselves from torture. An entire province had been stripped of inhabitants and given them to occupy; Greeks, French, Italians, Spanish, Dutch and others. They, and the black troops, were Ismail's favorites.

On the next day, as though in answer to his lie, Forbes ran into two of them, an Englishman and a Sicilian. The two were alone, riding for Meknes; he tried to steer clear of them, but they ran him down. They were cruel, bitter, hard men of wrecked lives and blasted future, and the Englishman was by far the worse of the two. He had a pistol, and his sharp eye perceived the truth.

"You're no Arab, by the way you ride," said he, hauling out his pistol. "And no Berber either. Ha, comrade! Here's an escaped slave!"

"Have ye no bowels o' mercy?" spat out Forbes in English,

seeing the dark Sicilian reaching for sword or knife, and the pistol cocked. "Let be, and go your way; the Lord will bless you for it."

"And have that jabbering Italian yonder peach on me? Not much," said the other coolly. "English yourself, are you? Scotch, by the burr of your tongue. Turn around and ride with us, and lucky we don't make you walk with your hands tied to our stirrups!"

FORBES UTTERED a groan of despair, and the two laughed heartily. In the midst, they ceased to laugh; Forbes launched himself from the saddle, caught the Englishman about the body, and fell with him in the dust. The pistol missed fire, but the knife drove home.

The Sicilian dismounted and ran in upon them with drawn sword. Out of the dust and blood rose Forbes, hurling the pistol into the dark face, following it with his knife. The sword caught him over the scalp, but his point slid home again; a brief and savage blur of fighting figures that ended with two men dead, who were better dead perhaps, and Forbes with three horses and a gash over his skull.

It was this wound that did for him.

His own horse was the best of the three. With it, with the pistol and powder and ball, with more looted food, he pressed on hard and fast. He got into the hills, and there made himself a camp near water, for fever was in his wound and he could scarcely keep his feet, and his saddle not at all.

Two days he lay all but senseless, helpless, in delirium. He came to himself, weak but clear-headed; he was on the mend. The horse had wandered away. No matter! There were the hills, and there wound a dusty ribbon of road piercing them—the road to the sea!

Food heartened him, water did not lack, and he remained here another day to gain strength. Hope grew in him. He had passed the worst barriers now. By following that road of nights and lying hid by day, he would reach the coast; he had food and weapons and a little money. His future was assured, provided he could steal some sort of boat at the coast and get to sea.

Grimly, he struggled on and on.

DAYS PASSED. Afoot, he reached the mountains; gaunt, hawk-eyed, alert, worn to skin and bone, he got through them. Starving now, he killed a Berber shepherd and drank the blood of a slaughtered sheep, and staggered on, hiding by day, footing it by night. He followed trails that ever led him northward and a little west.

Came the day when, crouching amid thorn-brush and cactus as a train of horsemen passed, he heard their talk and learned that he was in the territory of the Pasha of Tetuan. This clarified everything for him. That afternoon, late, he had his first glimpse of the sea—a blue glitter of water, far away but certain.

He sat down, then, and shook with passionate sobs until tears were exhausted.

All that night he went on his way, spurred by a fervor that surmounted weariness and bloody feet and hunger. That over-heard conversation had changed all his plans. Now he need not worry about the last barrier. He was close to the Spanish terri-tory of Ceuta. He had only to reach the Spanish lines, to be safe for ever. The joyous thrill of it pounded in his veins and pulsed through his whole being. Safe!

Toward dawn, he heard the dogs of a village barking, and began to pick his way around the place. It was no easy matter, for the fields were marked out by hedges of enormous cactus, hundreds of years old. The dogs, aware of him, kept up their noise. The false dawn was graying the east when, in avoiding a cactus-patch, Forbes lost his footing and tumbled into a rocky pit.

He struck headfirst. His half-healed wound was opened, and he lay senseless. When he wakened to consciousness, he was lying in the village, with chains on his wrist and feet. His escape had come to its end.

WITH THIS, old Manning's fingers fell, as though his story had come to an end. He leaned back wearily, with an air of finality, and closed his eyes.

Cotterel stared at him, with a look of shock in his eyes, then spoke.

"But look here! You've not finished? What became of Forbes?"

Manning looked up, and his hands moved. "I don't know what became of him. He was taken back to Meknes, that's all we know. Probably he lies in those enormous rotting walls today."

"But still I don't understand." Cotterel had come out of his savage, hostile mood. The abrupt finish of the story, the transition from suspense and triumph ahead, to frightful disaster, had wakened his brain. He was more like his usual self now, and Manning, who had played for that very aim, was thankful to see it.

"What has that story got to do with me?" went on Cotterel, gripped by curiosity and interest. "I can see a certain analogy in the situation, yes. But I don't see where the escape of Forbes has anything to do with whatever try at a break I might make."

"On the contrary, it has everything to do with you," Manning replied. "I know you don't get the point, old man. I didn't want to make it too clear at first. I mentioned one thing that didn't occur to him, that never occurs to anyone in such a situation. It didn't occur to Suds Jackson when he made his successful break recently. It didn't occur to you, and naturally it wouldn't."

"Yes." Cotterel frowned. "I remember. What's that thing?"

"Wait!" Manning made a warning gesture and leaned forward, listening intently.

Cotterel could hear nothing. Yet through the murmurous silence of the prison, he realized the grapevine must be at work—the grapevine which carried news. Old Manning was aware of it, but Cotterel was not. It took years, instead of mere months, to be able to grasp the slight sounds, the telegraphic sounds which eluded even the ears of the prison guards.

Manning was getting something. A blaze came into his eyes,

his head jerked up, his lips moved soundlessly. Then he turned abruptly to Cotterel.

"Suppose you succeeded in making a break, son. You'd be about the best-known man in America, from the police standpoint. There'd be no safety anywhere for you."

Cotterel gestured disdainfully.

"I don't care about that. I'm going to be free again, if only for a day or so! I crave the free air. Just to stand once on a hillside under the blue sky, and be free!"

"Precisely; that proves the point I'm trying to make." Manning smiled slightly. "You think of freedom day and night, just as Forbes did. The one thing that never occurred to him, that has never occurred to you either, the unseen possibility that never occurred to Suds Jackson when he succeeded in his break! I don't mean the fear of death—"

He broke off, and then resumed abruptly, his fingers flying fast.

"Do you know what I just got from the grapevine? That Suds Jackson will be back tomorrow. He's been recaptured, and alive."

"Oh, hell! That's too bad." Cotterel caught his breath sharply. "Oh, I see! You think that possibility hadn't occurred to me?"

"No, not at all," said Manning's fingers. "Think of Forbes in the moment when he passed again between the gates of Meknes and into the slave prison. Think of Suds Jackson, when tomorrow he's brought back inside these gates. That's the unseen possibility; the inevitable moment, not of death, but of return."

Cotterel's eyes dilated. "Oh, I see—I see! You're right. The moment of return, of being brought back here—"

"Just that," said Manning.

COTTEREL LOWERED his head. A little shiver passed through him as he sat motionless and silent. After a time he looked up, met the gaze of Manning, and wiped fine perspiration from his forehead.

"I get the point," he said suddenly. "I—I—damn it, you're

right! I guess I've been the world's prize fool, Manning. Just the bare thought of that moment of return gives me the creeps. I'm sorry for everything I said. Forgive me, won't you?"

Their hands met in understanding.

THE FACT UNKNOWN

A CIVIL WAR PRISON IS THE SCENE OF THIS MOVING AND DRAMATIC
STORY—THE SEVENTH IN THIS "STRANGE ESCAPES" SERIES.

"**A**LWAYS," SAID old Manning, speaking without a sound, "always there is a fact unknown This is true of every man doomed to die. It may be some fact within himself, or outside of himself. Often, indeed, it may prove to be a friend known. A fact, a friend—these things are hard to define. Friends and facts are two different things, you say? I'm not so sure."

Cotterel stared moodily, glumly, at his cell-mate. The prison was silent. A guard paced by their cell door and glanced in at the two men sitting there, and went his way. Even in moments such as this, when no talk was allowed, these two men could talk freely, with no covert mutterings.

Old Manning had a touch of the mystic about him, thought Cotterel as he stared. Too much so at times; he was hard to understand. An old man, fragile, a delicate artist—a forger, in fact.

Cotterel was in for life, for a crime he had never committed. To him these months of prison had been undiluted agony; he was young, and life meant much to him. He was given to moods of rebellion, black despairing moods. Only old Manning, at such times, had held him from frenzied folly. The two were friends, and Manning had come to feel a real and deep affection for the younger man. Cotterel knew it, and valued it beyond words. It was the one thing left him in the world.

"A fact unknown? A friend? What are you driving at, anyway?" he demanded.

Manning regarded the younger man steadily, with a worried air. Then his fingers, the slender fingers of an artist an engraver, a forger of bank-notes, made reply. Manning had this peculiarity: he was dumb. Cotterel, in these months of close association, had readily picked up the sign language, and could use it fluently, although as a rule he spoke naturally, for Manning's ears were good.

"What's on your mind?" Manning spelled out the words, an expression of concern in his face. "I know you're innocent; you were sent here wrongly—"

"That's just it!" burst forth Cotterel, if such a term could be applied to his agonized finger-play. "I've been put in hell for life, and who gives a damn?"

"Wait," intervened the older man cynically. " 'Life' doesn't mean *life*, really; perhaps twenty years—"

Manning accomplished his sly intent. Cotterel, despite his situation, rallied in a heated argument.

"The point is," he concluded, "that twenty years might as well be all of life. No one gives a hang. I've nobody, except the woman I love. She has no money, no influence. What will have become of her, after twenty years? What will become of me, old, broken, wrecked? And all because of something I did not do."

"I know," Manning returned. "Your trial was a miscarriage of justice. Yet, as I said, there's always a fact unknown. It should be the mental alleviation, the one last hope, of every man in your fix. No matter what the fact is—whether sympathy in the breast of one juror, of one faithful friend; no matter if the man himself cannot believe it possible, can see no shred of hope at all."

"Hope!" Cotterel's face was drawn and bitter. "There's no such thing—for me, anyhow."

"THAT'S WHAT Bannister thought," said Manning on nimble fingers. "He was more correct than you in the premise, for he was up against the only form of abstract justice that we have in America: military law."

"Who the devil was Bannister?"

"Safe enough to talk now.... Donald,
old man, don't you know me?"

"A Virginian. A tall, dark, grave young man; he had everything in life to live for—money and love and rank and ambition.
In one moment, all this was stripped from him, and he stood
face to face with inexorable death—condemned, although innocent, to the ignominy of the noose. He had no particle of hope
from any quarter."

Again the older man had achieved his shrewd purpose. Cotterel was frowning at him, intently, with mind turned to a man in worse case than himself; the congested lobe of his brain, inflamed by thought and worry in his own behalf, was relieved as other lobes took up the labor and bent themselves to work on the case of Bannister.

"Is this some of your antique history, like the story of the dog Azo?" * he demanded with a trace of scorn in his face.

"Not so antique!" And Manning smiled gently. "It happened in what was then known as Western Virginia, when the Army of the Potomac faced Lee across the Rapidan, back in 1863, Bannister was a captain of cavalry in Stonewall Jackson's corps,"

"Oh! Civil War stuff!" muttered Cotterel under his breath.

Manning blazed up. "The most truly American stuff you'll ever hear! Stuff instinct with every American virtue and fault! It is a civil war that brings out, through hatred and the most ruthless enmity, the finest qualities of any race. For hatred, like an alloy, dies into a firmly welding content of the finest steel. Bannister, like so many others, was one of a divided family—"

Manning was silent, thoughtful, in repose, for a long moment; then his deft, agile fingers began to move once more.

BANNISTER HAD a younger brother, whom he had not seen in four years. The boy had worshiped him in the early days; then had been appointed to West Point; and when the war broke, had gone slap into the Union Army. Where he was, what had become of him, Bannister had not the least idea.

And now look at Bannister in his cell, a plastered cell in a stout little jail, well back of the Union lines. A brick and iron jail, solidly built, with escape impossible; all about it, in the jail yard, were stationed the men of the quartermaster's corps; the wall beyond was manned by sentries, the town streets beyond were filled with Union troops. Only the worst criminals were confined here—and men sentenced to death, like Bannister.

---

* *See "Four Out of Bondage."*

He had been caught back of the lines in Federal uniform; no two ways about that. The woman he loved, who lived in Fredericksburg, lay seriously ill; Bannister had stolen through the lines to see her. And he had been caught. He had gambled all, and had lost.

HATRED RAN high in those days. Yanks and Johnnies shared a bitter and abiding hatred. Spies were everywhere; when caught, they were dealt with by the rules of war. And Bannister, caught and recognized and haled before military law, was sentenced to be hanged.

Now, in his cell, he mentally reviewed his hopeless case. The advocate given him, an officer of rank, had believed his plain story, had accepted his word of honor that he was no spy; no one else had believed or accepted it. An appeal had been made to General Hooker. Until the answer came, he could not be certain when the execution would take place; but the delay held no hope whatever. Here was one of those terrible cases where all the open evidence was damning, where a man might desperately lie to save his neck—where even a lie would not be dishonor, since it would be in the service of a cause. Bannister knew this only too well.

His inner agony was frightful, but he gave no token of it except the drawn look in his harshly chiseled features. He had an old razor, and managed to shave daily—a rather rare thing, since most men were of necessity bearded in those days. As he sat, the distant mutter of artillery shook the air, hour after hour....

To die by the noose! To die, quickly and shamefully, when Hooker's reply arrived! He could think of nothing else. Escape? It was impossible. He was well watched. His cell was searched each morning, when he was led out with the others under heavy guard of shotted guns, for daily exercise.

He sat there, sunk in hopeless despair, waiting. This was the horrible part of it: nothing to do but wait. Any occupation might have helped him mentally, but he had none. He had begged for even manual work, and it was curtly denied by his guards.

The Commandant would not permit it. The Commandant—the accursed Commandant! He ruled that little jail with an iron rule. Bannister had twice seen him at a distance, a bearded, erect man in his blue officer's uniform. The Commandant would hang him in a few days more. That, he thought bitterly, would finish him with this blasted Commandant!

He was in shirt and Union blue trousers, just as he had been captured. With a weary sigh, he turned to the supper that had been put inside his barred

In stark incredulity, he stared.

and massive door. Beans, potatoes, a slab of sow-belly, a tin cup of coffee, a slab of still warm corn-bread, a wooden spoon—a fine and plentiful meal, by wartime standards. He picked up the slab of corn-bread, and it fell apart in his hand.

Blankly, in sheer stark incredulity, he stared. A thin, tiny file of steel, a scrap of paper, folded.

The blood rushed through his brain, in sudden comprehension. He swiftly slid the tiny file into his boot-top and opened

the scrap of paper. A few words were printed on it in pencil—
printed, to avoid betrayal of handwriting if intercepted.

Don't Shave. Waiting Midnight Tomorrow Your Window.

Bannister wet his lips. A rattle of bolts at his door. He started,
and shot the scrap of paper into his mouth, just as the door
opened and a guard looked in.

"Tray ain't ready, Cap'n?"

"Haven't had the heart to eat," said Bannister, feigning dejection to conceal his hammering pulses and inward excitement.
"I'll get at it right now."

With a grumble, the guard slammed and bolted the massive
door.

Bannister attacked his meal, avidly and wolfishly. The words
of that note, with all they implied, burned into his consciousness. Some friend unknown, some Southern sympathizer, was
here and at work. Perhaps one of the cooks—yes, that must be it!

Outside his window, tomorrow midnight? Perhaps, after all,
one of the teamsters from the quartermaster's wagons parked in
the jail yard. That would be more like it. Waiting, with clothes
for him, with help!

Therefore, by tomorrow midnight, he must file his way
through those window bars. He had the night, luckily, all tomorrow, tomorrow evening. To file even soft iron is slow work and
laborious.

So his mind rioted, while he ate, and darkness deepened. He
carefully adjusted the wooden spoon under his heel, and broke
it. When the guard came in, bringing a light, and lighted the
candle allotted the prisoner, Bannister pointed to the broken
pieces on the floor. He picked up the bowl of the spoon and
tossed it on the tray.

"Sorry," he said carelessly. "I dropped the spoon in the dark
and stepped on it."

"You'll eat with your fingers tomorrow, I reckon," growled

the guard, who was a savage soul. "That is, if you ain't hung tomorrow."

Taking the tray, the man departed. Bannister waited, tensed, breathless, as the bolts shot home in the door. Then he relaxed in sharp, untold relief. Stooping, his trembling fingers picked up the shaft of the spoon; no attention had been paid to it, luckily.

He sat down and fell to work, glancing now and again at the window. It was of fair size, perhaps eight feet above the ground. Three bars traversed it in each direction—bars of flat strap iron, twisted, set solidly into the bricks. If he cut three at the side and two at the bottom, he might be able to bend out the whole thing and squirm through the opening. His brain flew back to stories he had heard—dirt and bread-crumbs filling the filed cuts, so they could not be observed.

Under flying fingers, he finished his preliminary job. To use that little file, so rapidly, so continuously, would be tremendously difficult; he had appreciated this almost from the first. But with a handle on it, the task would be lightened. Hence the shaft of the wooden spoon. He unraveled threads from his shirt, from his stout blue woolen trousers, which were ripped in places.

Threads, not strips. His agile brain was sharply aware that many tiny threads make a more durable and stouter binding than larger strips. Around and around, endlessly, he wrapped and tied. The file was bound to the wooden handle, a couple of inches protruding, and that was plenty just now. He could change it later if necessary.

So he fell at last to the actual work on the bars, after pinching out his candle.

HIS ONE fear of possible discovery came from outside his window. Men were all over the jail yard, squatted around camp-fires, telling yarns, drinking, singing songs; but if any approached closely, they would hear the rasping file.

There was little danger from the guard, who looked in occasionally; when this happened, the first noise of the bolts rasping back sent Bannister flopping on his couch, apparently sound asleep.

Hour passed into hours. Cramped at the window, he worked steadily. His first fervor died out after a time; he was appalled to realize the horribly slow progress he made. If he had possessed a week in which to work, all would have been lovely. The stories about prisoners who had worked months and years with make-shift implements, flocked into his mind with ghastly, mocking contrast. He had twenty-four hours—and perhaps would not have that, if the answer came from Hooker. That his appeal would be denied, was practically certain.

IT WAS long after midnight change of guard when one bar was through. The dawn was graying when the second yielded. Two only. Haggard, weary, his fingers raw, his hand-muscles so strained and aching that they were almost useless, he contemplated the three remaining bars with sinking heart. Before the next midnight they must be cut—and with daylight, he would not dare run the risk of being seen at the window, working.

Disheartened, a thousandfold more despairing than before, he managed to fill the cuts with dirt gathered from the floor. His file hidden in his boot, he dropped on his cot and slumbered like a man dead.

Later in the morning, the guard stirred him roughly awake, for inspection. This was casual enough. Bannister polished off his breakfast, was marched around and around the yard for exercise, was locked up again. The exercise period ended early—a drizzle of rain was falling.

The drizzle became a deluge, with thunder booming overhead and drowning out the guns that muttered along the Wilderness front.

At this, a feverish hope leaped in the prisoner's heart. That storm of rain kept all loungers away in the yard; he dared to work again, with strips of cloth from his shirt wound about his raw fingers. And in the light of day, he found the work easier; besides, he had learned the knack of it.

In between the squalls of rain, he desisted, but taking no chances; when men muffled in greatcoats passed his window, he drew away hastily. As the early daylight waned, he shook the bar and shook it again, put his grip to it—and it broke.

Two bars remained to cut.

Evening drew down. The worst of the rain was over; it had settled now into an intermittent drizzle. A wet disagreeable night, and nothing could have suited Bannister's purpose better. His supper over, he was hard at work when the rasping bolts warned him. He dropped everything, and was lying on his cot when an officer entered with a lantern and a guard. He was roused, a black stubble of unshaven beard blurring his features.

"I have a letter here to read you—"

It burned into him as he stood at attention—burned with scathing phrases. General Joe Hooker had no use for spies, and said so…. Immediate execution—to be hanged at daybreak. He would be roused an hour beforehand. A chaplain would be sent him.

He was alone again in darkness, alone with destiny. The appeal denied! Well, to the devil with it, and Joe Hooker to boot!

A shaky laugh was in his brain and on his lips, as he crept back to the window and took up his file anew. To be hanged at daybreak? Well, his unknown friend had saved him from that, at least. He might stop a bullet, but he would never be hanged now!

As his fingers pressed steel to iron, he fell to reflecting anew upon the identity of that unknown friend outside. Some teamster, hardly a doubt of that, pressed into service and hating the Federals secretly. Perhaps, of course, one of the cooks, but more likely a teamster from among the wagons here at hand.

Once in the yard here, what about the wall and the sentries? Well, time enough to think about that, and the town streets beyond, with Yanks everywhere. If his unknown friend could provide garments for him, some way of passing the wall or the sentries might also be provided.

"Wait and see!" he told himself, as the iron and the file shred-

"I have a letter here to read you." General Hooker
had no use for spies, and said so.... Immediate
execution—to be hanged at daybreak.

ded his finger-ends. "With an unknown friend, anything is
possible!"

He worked frantically, resolutely.

TEN O'CLOCK, by the sentries' calls. The iron twist yielded under his bleeding hands; one remained. He attacked it without pause. Two hours.

Fatigue, lack of sleep, weary hands—nothing mattered now. He was to hang with the dawn, if he remained here, and he revolted against that dog's death, recoiled with all his Virginian heart and soul. Better by far to stop the hot lead of sentries in some wild and hopeless dash for liberty! Once out of here, he was assured of that more kindly fate, at least....

Rasp and rasp; pause, with fingers aching. Wet the iron. Rasp and rasp again. Change position, pause, work the fatigued, worn fingers, and then to rasping again with teeth set hard and iron will spurring the failing muscles.

Eleven o'clock. Outside in the yard, no fires or lights; the wagons empty, save for teamsters asleep in them. The rain slackening, a breath of wet sweet wind from the countryside, then gathering rain once more. A perfect night, perfect!

He worked on and on. He could feel the little wedge of nothingness as the file bit deeper and deeper. In a frenzy, he felt the handle coming loose, tore it free, and put the new and sharper unused edges of the file to work; he toiled in a fury of hurried heart and gritting teeth and bleeding fingers.

Midnight; the guard was being relieved.

Still the iron held, but only by a shred. Gasping, he gripped it, bent his weight against it—*crack!* The bar gave.

Finished! For a moment he hung there, sobbing in breath after breath of relief. Then, standing on his cot, he braced himself and leaned his weight again. As he had calculated, the remaining bars bent well enough to serve his objective.

Farther and farther out he bent them; then desisted, panting. The way was open. He was as good as free this moment. Yet midnight had come, and passed, with no sign from his unknown friend. A squad of men went tramping past in the mud and cinders of the yard. As their slogging tread died out, a voice spoke softly.

"Bannister?"

"All set. Shall I come out?"

"Quickly."

A thick, gruff voice, quite strange to him. Oddly enough, at this instant Bannister hesitated, held back mentally. A frightful conjecture broke upon him; had this escape been arranged so that he might be shot down? He had heard of some such thing being worked. Then he laughed, and swung himself at the window. What matter? Better a bullet than the hangman's noose!

He forced himself out, squeezing past the cut bars that scraped his body. He let himself go any way at all, careless of how he landed, and came down with a flop that knocked the wind out of him.

IN THE darkness, a dim black figure loomed over him, helped him up.

"Hurt? No? Here!"

The gruff words were curt. Bannister gasped breath into his jolted lungs as garments were shoved at him. For the moment, the rain had ceased. The wet air was sodden, dense with humidity.

Garments—a dark shirt, a coat, a muffling army overcoat. As he struggled into them, Bannister eyed the vaguely black figure beside him. To see any details of the man was quite impossible.

"Who are you, anyhow?" he demanded.

"No talk," came the response. "Here."

Bannister took the black slouch hat thrust at him, and pulled it over his head. The coat was around him, the collar up about his face.

"Ready? Come along. Keep close," came the order, and the other man started away, straight for the entrance gate. Bannister came up to him, touched him on the arm and halted him, with a low word.

"Tell me—"

"Shut up!" The response was savage and curt. "No talk."

The voice of a man at high tension, keyed up to taut nerves; Bannister, realizing his own folly in trying to learn who this companion was, muttered an apology and fell a step behind.

They came to the gate, where a lantern swung. Bannister found himself detained by a touch, as the guard was turned out. His companion advanced a step or two and spoke with the corporal in charge of the squad, who saluted briskly. Ah! An officer, then!

He could not see the man's face at all; a sword-scabbard flashed beneath the greatcoat. He could not hear the low, muttered words. The corporal saluted again, and ordered the gate swung open.

"Everything quiet, sir," he said. "You're going down the street? There's a picket blocking it, fifty feet outside; they'll know you, of course."

Oh! Bannister heard these words clearly enough. No teamster, no cook, but an officer, and some well-known officer, at that. The mystery of it enveloped him, staggered him. An officer, a Union officer, arranging his escape? It was incredible.

Something more incredible still lay ahead of him, as he followed the other outside. His companion caught his arm.

"Silence, on your life! Keep close."

With this, the Federal officer swung straight ahead. A fire glowed dimly, protected from the rain and wind. Lanterns bobbed. Men were moving about. Obviously, the street here was blocked by this picket. Bannister, with sharp realization, perceived that he would never have been able to pass, alone.

His companion, who had escorted him out of the prison yard, was now, obviously, seeing him safe through this final danger. Or was there a trap in it? Utterly illogical as the thought was, Bannister none the less felt it pluck at him.

THE RAIN was beginning to drizzle afresh. A sentry halted the two. Bannister tried to obey the order and keep close to his

The bar gave....
He braced himself;
farther and farther
out he bent the
remaining bars.

companion; but the latter, after a glance at two officers coming to interrogate him, uttered a word.

"Wait."

With this word, he stepped forward to meet the two officers. There was a quick exchange of greetings, a hand-grip, and the three moved off to one side, talking together. Evidently, once more, this companion of his was well known, Bannister reflected. He waited, immobile, drawing the coat collar closer about his face. The guard ignored him; but his glances flitted about, taking in every detail in case something went wrong and he had to leg it down the street. A dark, unlit street, deserted at this hour of the night, all lights extinguished. A man could hide well enough, he thought, somewhere among the houses of the town.

The three officers seemed to be discussing him, for one gestured toward him. Again he felt uneasy; again the notion of a trap recurred to his mind. He tried hard to catch some of the talk, but could not; the three figures were indistinct enough at best, and the dreary rain-patter in the puddles obscured all sounds of speech.

"Well, good night to you!" One of the officers clapped his guide on the shoulder. The two turned back to their warm shelter. A guard with a lantern appeared.

"Come along!"

At the gruff command, Bannister obeyed. His companion said something to the guard, who halted with a clumsy salute. From his lantern, a glimmer of light lit the face of Bannister's companion, lit it from the side.

"You don't want me to light you through the mud?" said the guard. "Very good, sir. A good night to you. We'll be watching for your return, Commandant."

Bannister, already stepping forward, was checked as by a hand thrust at his chest.

Commandant! That word, that flash of the guard's lantern on the bearded profile of his companion, struck Bannister absolutely dumb. The prison Commandant himself! Hot suspicion flamed through his brain. What devil's trickery was this—perhaps to get him swiftly shot? As he hesitated and drew back, the other spoke gruffly.

"Come along, come along!"

In the rain and mud and darkness, Bannister swung into step again. Then his companion halted, swung around, gripped him by the shoulders.

"Safe enough to talk now.... Donald, old man, don't you know me?"

Bannister quivered. The low, laughing voice—

"Why, Jack, boy!" he gasped. "It can't be you—it's impossible!"

The other laughed; they clung together for a moment, until Bannister drew back. This bearded officer, the boy so long lost to sight, his own brother!

A dim figure loomed over him. "Hurt? No? Here!" The gruff words were curt.

"But Jack, what the devil does it all mean?" he demanded, bewildered. "If you're the commandant, why haven't you come near me, sent me word?"

"Didn't dare do it, Donald," the other rejoined. "I couldn't raise your hopes; I had to keep our relationship quiet. Nobody suspected, in spite of the names being alike. All hands have been too cursed busy to think. I knew it was you, of course. I went over the records of your case. You had given your word of honor that you weren't spying—that was good enough for me, Don. Nobody else believed it, but I believed it."

"Thanks, old fellow," said Bannister quietly. "Lord, but it's good to see you again, to find you alive and well! So you contrived this escape?"

The other grunted. "More than that. There was no use appealing to Hooker; it was only too certain what his answer would be. I took a chance and telegraphed direct to Lincoln—to Old Abe. I staked my honor on yours, my faith on yours; asked him for a pardon, on condition you'd not bear arms against us further—the honor of a Virginia gentleman, Don."

Bannister caught his breath.

"Good Lord, Jack! What did he say?"

"Nothing," rejoined the other bitterly. "No reply. Yesterday afternoon, I received a communication from Hooker, denying your appeal and ordering you executed at once. Well—I tell you, for a while I was like a crazy man!" As he spoke, agitation filled his voice. "Then I thought of the way—the escape, I lost Hooker's letter and took a chance on getting hell for it, later. I got the file and message to you. I didn't dare lose the letter longer than a day, you see. I found it again this afternoon. You know the rest—to be hanged at daylight. Meantime, all was well, I trusted, with your escape. So that's the story. Now, I want your promise not to bear arms against us further. It'll salve my conscience for what I've done, Don; brother or no brother, by God, it's not been easy!"

"You have my word," said Bannister quietly. Their hands gripped.

"Thanks, Don," came the reply. "Now, we'll go down to the next street. I have a horse ready and waiting. The password is *Gideon*. I've a pass written out for you, besides."

"And no answer from Lincoln, eh?"

"None. Of course, that was a desperate chance— Good Lord! Stand quiet!"

Bobbing lanterns, clicking, mud-throwing hoofs, several riders coming hastily upon them, with no chance for evasion. They drew against a house-wall, the Commandant shielding Bannister's figure. The dancing rays of a lantern touched them, shouts rang out. One of the riders dismounted with a salute.

"Here y'are, Commandant!" he exclaimed. "I seen it was danged important, so I come on the run to find you. Just come in over the wire—wrote it down myself."

The Union officer took the slip of paper. A lantern was held close as he read it.

"Thank God!" he said in a low voice. "Donald—the answer from Washington! Lincoln accepts my plea, orders you released—"

ALL THE night scene faded and was gone in a tramp of feet. Cotterel was in the prison cell again, guards at the door, a rough voice snapping out an order:

"Thirty-seven-fifteen!" That was old Manning's prison number. "Thirty-seven-fifteen! You're wanted at the Warden's office. Step out!"

Cotterel stared up blankly. Manning rose, gestured assent, and in passing, touched his cheek with those slender, deft fingers: A caress, a farewell, an assurance what was it? Just a friendly touch, perhaps.

Alone, Cotterel sat staring. Something wrong? Such a summons to the Warden's office meant something tremendous, something weighty, in the air. He sat in growing suspense and anxiety; yet despite his tension, his mind dwelt upon the story that Manning had just told him.

Now he perceived what Manning must have meant by his earlier mention of a "fact unknown." Bannister had never dreamed, of course, that the prison Commandant was his own brother, planning for him, hoping for him, pleading and working for his life. The thing must have broken upon his spirit like a flash of lightning across the sky.

"But that's just it—there was a different case," he muttered, falling into instant and more profound despair. "Nothing like that for me. I've no family, nobody. The woman I love is helpless. These days, we can't expect such miracles as a pardon from the President." A hollow laugh escaped him. "The President! Fat chance, these days. What the devil did Manning mean by telling me all that yarn, anyhow? I know better—"

HE LOOKED up, came to his feet. Manning was being ushered into the cell again. The older man was joyous, beaming. His flashing fingers broke into instant swift speech.

"Cotterel! Remember what I said—about the fact unknown? It was true. The Warden said I might tell you myself. I went to him awhile back; I told him everything about your case. He just got a letter about it. That's why he sent for me—"

"The Warden?" blurted Cotterel. "My case? What the hell is it to him?"

"Well, it's a lot to me." And Manning laughed silently, "I can do nothing for myself, but I have friends outside. The Warden let me appeal to them. They went to the judges, to the Governor. Old man, it's happened! You're to have a new trial; your case is to be re-opened—and you know what that'll mean! All this hell is ended for you, my boy."

Cotterel sank on his cot, as though beneath actual physical impact. He drew a deep breath; his face sank in his hands, and a sob shook him.

But old Manning, beside him, leaned forward and touched his cheek gently, caressingly, with the deft nimble fingers that would never forge again.

THE WAY TO FREEDOM

TWO STORIES EACH COME TO A DRAMATIC CLIMAX HERE:
ONE THE STORY OF THE STRANGE ESCAPE OF A BRITON FROM
FRANCE; AND THE OTHER—BUT READ FOR YOURSELF.

THE TRUSTY guiding Cotterel—who required no guide—looked at him with unfeigned envy. "How does it feel to be back in stir, but a free man?"

Cotterel laughed. "Not so good, if you want to know. I had to come back, to see Manning. The Warden says he's not so good."

The trusty shook his head. "Nope. They took old Finger Tricks to the hospital yesterday. He went to pieces after you left. I guess he just don't want to live. There's the doc now. He can take you along."

The prison doctor shook hands with Cotterel. They all knew him here, knew he had been here for months, knew he had been found guiltless and pardoned out. They all had warm looks for him.

"Come along." The doctor nodded. "You have permission, of course—oh, as long as you like! Good. You'll cheer the old fellow up. Can you talk with him?"

"I was his cell-mate for months," said Cotterel simply.

Finger Tricks—a good name for the old forger, a doubly good nickname. He was in for life, and it would not be long now. In a bad way, said the doctor. What his lungs needed was Arizona air, high and dry. He was in hospital merely for tests, not because of disability; not yet.

Cotterel shivered a little. Then his shoulders squared, and he smiled once more, gayly, hopefully, cheerfully; old Manning must be cheered up....

They were alone together in the big ward; no other patients here, as it chanced. Prepared as he was, Cotterel was shocked by the change in his old friend. Manning's gray features were lined and drawn and tired; his sunken eyes were less bright than of old. His long, slender fingers, the fingers of a born artist, the fingers of a forger, were nimble as ever, however.

The joy in his face, his eyes, his hands, was a thing electric.

"Heard a few days ago you were not so well off," said Cotterel, sitting down. Smoking was allowed here. He produced cigarettes.

"I'm done," said Manning. "It's the finish, boy."

His fingers spoke for him. During many years Manning had been dumb, due to throat trouble, and Cotterel, his cell-mate, had learned the finger-talk; it had come in handy many times when no talking was allowed. He did not need to use it now, however.

"Manning, you did a lot for me when I was in here," he said abruptly. "You did every possible thing one man can do for another."

"Steered you right," said the deft fingers.

"More than that. You showed me the real man inside of you; we got pretty close, in those days. There's only one way I can repay all you've done for me—that's by getting you out of here."

Manning opened his mouth and emitted a hoarse, almost soundless cackle.

"Escape? Me?" he said on his fingers. "Don't talk foolishness."

"And," said Cotterel, "while I was here and half out of my head, and thinking day and night of escape, you held me back with your wisdom. Your stories of other escapes. Did you ever hear of Sir Sydney Smith?"

Manning frowned. Well-educated, talented, versatile, Manning had been unable to escape his one weakness, the one great gift so terribly misused. He was a gentle, kindly man; his real affection had kept Cotterel from going mad in this same prison.

Now he said slowly:

"I vaguely recall the name; a British admiral, I think. Wasn't he the man who beat Napoleon at Acre and changed the whole destiny of the Corsican?"

Cotterel nodded, with a sudden flashing smile.

"So there's something I can teach you, is there?" he observed. "Yes, you've got the right man in mind. Sir Sydney was a brusque, forcible and forth-

Smith took the letter. "I'll read it when my parole is up," he said.

right seaman; also, he was a gentleman, willing to endanger his whole career to avoid dishonor. Well, he learned something when he was a young captain, the most dashing and popular captain in the fleet. He learned something that you should learn, that you must learn."

Manning smiled. "My friend," said his flying fingers, "I see that you're giving me a dose of my own medicine. Yes, I'm willing to learn. But nothing will do me any good now—nothing."

This evidence of a despondent, hopeless heart touched Cotterel deeply.

"That's what Sir Sydney felt too. Back in 1796, when the French Revolution had passed its bloodiest height, when the Directory was in power, when Bonaparte's star was rising brilliantly, Sir Sydney didn't know the lesson of the simplest way; but he learned it."

"The simplest way?" Manning's head came up. His sunken eyes searched Cotterel with sudden swift alertness. "You mean, of escape?"

"Precisely. And God helping me, I mean to teach you that lesson if I can," said Cotterel solemnly. "The simplest way! But let me tell you about Sir Sydney. He had led a boat raid far up the Seine River, into the very heart of France, when he was captured; with him was a French nobleman, the Marquis de Taifort, exiled and sentenced to death by the revolutionary government. Luckily, Taifort was not recognized by their captors; he adopted the position of Sir Sydney's servant and the fantastic dress of a jockey. As the jockey and valet, John, who pretended to speak little or no French, he remained with Sir Sydney. The ignorance of the French regarding English customs and manners was extreme; the people in power at that time, remember, were not people of education and knowledge.

"The Directory were overjoyed at Smith's capture. They declared him to be a spy and had him sent to Paris. There, for two years, he was most rigorously confined in the Temple, the former prison of the royal family. Every effort of the British Government to effect his release or exchange was flatly refused. But you must see those two men in their prison, in this historic and terrible Temple. It was a tiny place, able to hold only a very few prisoners—"

A TINY place indeed, a tower with a wall about it, six hundred years old; a tower and wall and garden, and outside it the city encroaching closely—noisome tenements, huddled old structures that housed workmen and loose women. A little tower, a hundred and fifty feet high, the last relic of the once glorious stronghold of the Templars.

Here, then, was Sir Sydney, in the second year of his captivity; a handsome, fluent, vivacious man of thirty, a man filled with the ardent flame of reckless adventure, and quartered in the very rooms from which Louis XVI had gone to death four years previously. With him was Taifort, his supposed valet, now passing by the name of John; a merry soul, gay and clever, a fascinating man liked by everyone, always wearing his extravagant costume of jockey's buckskin breeches and boots—facing immediate death if that disguise were penetrated.

Such men are not to be contained by iron bars.

DURING THE weary months they had planned escape with tortuous care.

Three other men confined in the Temple, dangerous royalists, had joined in the attempt. But one of them had turned traitor at the last moment. Now, in the high room whose barred window overlooked the street and the tenements opposite, Sir Sydney sat in the utmost dejection.

"No use," he said despondently. "Now they watch us more closely than ever; our every movement is noted; our very food is inspected. What was difficult before, has now become impossible."

The valet John, who had been sitting for a long time at the window, turned to him.

"Bah! Don't let them break your spirit, my friend. Look at me! They take me for a servant. They give me liberties. I can drink with the guards, eat in the kitchen, make love to the jailer's daughter! And she's not so bad, I give you my word. Something may yet come of it."

Sir Sydney's lips twitched.

"A good thing your wife's in England, you rascal!"

"Madame la Marquise," said John under his breath, "is sitting at a window opposite, looking at me."

Smith's head jerked up. Luckily, he was too astounded to speak, for at the moment steps sounded at the door. A guard had come to look in through the wicket at the two prisoners; they were watched at all times. When the steps retreated, Smith ventured a word.

"Is this a joke?"

"Come and see."

Smith sauntered to the window. It was midsummer, beastly hot, and flies were everywhere. Looking out and down at the houses opposite, his gaze came to rest upon a broken window at which sat a woman, knitting. She looked up, and made a gesture. Her face, despite the frowsy shawl which framed it, was intelligent, handsome, lovely. Smith made a gesture, and she replied.

"Go and enjoy yourself below,"
Smith murmured. "I'll think up
some way to communicate with her."

"Here, what are you doing?" The door was flung open, and a guard clumped in. "Whom are you looking at, there?"

Smith turned, with a smile, and pointed to the street where

children were playing. The surly guard looked down, and grunted.

"None of that. Trying to attract their attention, are you? Stop it."

Alone again, Smith looked at his companion. His dejection was gone. Hope had flared up anew; schemes, stratagems, possibilities, surged within him.

"Go and enjoy yourself down below," he murmured. "I'll think up some way to communicate with her. Ah! I have it! Call in the guard."

THE GUARD appeared promptly. Smith pointed to the two windows, and begged for some old newspapers with which to kill the flies that were abundant.

"Kill them with your hands like other people, aristocrat," guffawed the soldier. "A spy needn't be afraid to soil his hands!"

"Very well," said Sir Sydney, and going to the window, fell to work at the flies. "Ha! John, I've discovered a new amusement. Thanks, my good soldier, thanks!"

The guard laughed; John departed to the kitchen, and Sir Sydney went on with his amusement. Inside of an hour, he had reached an understanding with the woman at the window across the way.

Within three or four days, the two of them had formulated a code of signals which permitted exchange of messages.

So closely had houses encroached upon the Temple, that at one point outside the little garden where the prisoners took daily exercise, a narrow little street barely ten feet wide separated the old tenements from the nine-foot-thick wall. It was at this point the project of escape was aimed.

One afternoon as the prisoners, a scant half-dozen in all, were walking about the little garden, Smith stopped to converse with one of the others. Immediately a guard charged down upon them roughly, seized them, and shoved them apart.

"No talking allowed, you rascals!" he roared. "Keep apart, or back to your rooms you'll go!"

Smith, as he was shoved violently away from the other, felt the folded paper thrust into his hand by the guard, and slipped it out of sight.

Later he got a moment to look at the writing before chewing up the paper: That particular guard was bribed, and might perhaps be trusted. A tunnel was being dug beneath the street at the narrow point designated. It would be slow work; patience!

He told John, that night; the two men rejoiced together.

A VERY singular relation existed between Sir Sydney and the chief jailer, Lasne, who was a ferocious republican and an implacable prison chief, but who was accustomed to deal with the nobility. For the Englishman he had conceived a high respect, frequently inviting him to dinner—for which Smith paid well—and treating him with courtesy.

One hot, sweltering evening, Lasne astonished his prisoner.

"It is insufferable here, monsieur. If I might have your word of honor not to so much as think of escape, I'll conduct you past the guards and give you an hour on the boulevards."

Smith's jaw fell, till he perceived that the offer was serious.

"Upon my word of honor!" he said. "I'll not even think of escape."

Fifteen minutes later he was wandering the streets of Paris, free.

Incredible as it may seem, this offer was repeated more than once. Orders came every now and then to redouble the severity of the prison regulations, and Lasne obeyed them harshly. None the less, he allowed Sir Sydney an hour or two of absolute freedom, always upon the same promise.

One evening as Smith strolled at liberty, a man came up to him, addressed him by name, stating he was from the Marquise de Taifort and wished to speak with him.

"That is impossible," said Sir Sydney. "I can communicate only from within the Temple—I have given my word."

"Then take this letter, read it, give me an answer."

Smith took the letter and pocketed it. "I'll read it when my parole is up, and give a reply in the usual way," he said, and turned back.

A man capable of such quixotic honor would be capable of anything. Lasne knew this very well, and made up for his periods of indulgence by redoubled severity when Smith was not on parole.

WEEKS PASSED. By means of the bribed guard and the window-signals, Smith was kept in touch with the progress of the work across the way, proceeding slowly but surely. The Marquise was in touch with several royalist agents, who had flung themselves into the task of freeing the prisoners of the Temple.

A charming young woman with a child, who had numerous gentleman callers, leased the entire building opposite the garden wall. Her callers came frequently and remained long, which would certainly have attracted unfavorable attention anywhere else in the world; revolutionary Paris, however, had discarded all moral and other inhibitions.

These callers were or had been gentlemen, which was a very bad thing for the enterprise in hand. However ardent or patriotic a gentleman may be, when it comes to digging a tunnel from a cellar beneath a street and under a wall on the other side, he is extremely liable to error, as any ditch-digger knows. There are occasional advantages in not being a gentleman, in the world of practical affairs.

The tunnel lengthened, and there was no suspicion. Sir Sydney, over on the other side of the wall, was filled with hope and eagerness. His valet John, however, was rather skeptical.

"If you can get word to them," he advised, "tell them to put a mason on the job, even at the risk of raising suspicion."

Smith managed the message, and the Marquise, at her broken window opposite, signaled that it would be done; also that the tunnel was nearly finished, and would be broken through the

next evening. Be ready to escape at once!

Here, then, came in sight the end of these long weeks of suspense. One more day! Then escape into the seething turmoil of Paris, disguise, evasion to the frontier, and rescue! Two years of imprisonment, of harsh treatment lightened only by occasional favors, were at an end. The volatile Smith could hardly contain himself.

NEXT MORNING, in the cellar of the house across the way, a mason was brought into the affair, properly blinded by gold. He consulted with the gentleman laborers, and gave his opinion that while their tunnel was the proper length, he thought it ran too low in the ground. He was promptly engaged to work all day on the job and bring it to a proper finish—but

The mason, whether by design or accident, had pierced through the wall!

not, of course, to pierce through the other side. That must be reserved for the hours of darkness.

So the mason fell to work. Hours later, he came upon stone, as he worked at the end of the tunnel, and began to remove the stone. It did not occur to anyone concerned that the tunnel, instead of being too low, might be too high.

Smith, that afternoon, was taking his exercise in the garden with the other prisoners, under the eye of watchful guards. One of these guards was stationed beside the high wall that closed off the street. The burly fellow, leaning on his musket, was drawing comfortably at his clay pipe, when something scratched on the wall beside him. He glanced at the wall, and his jaw actually dropped; his eyes bulged out, and he let fall his pipe with one low oath of dismayed stupefaction.

For, untouched by human hands, moved by some invisible power, that nine-foot stone wall seemed all a-crawl! A bit of rock was dislodged and fell at his feet. Then another. The *tap-tap-tap* of a hammer was heard. Then a whole chunk of rubble fell away.

At the wild, startled yell of the guard, Sir Sydney perceived the frightful truth. The mason, whether by design or accident, had pierced through the wall!

The alarm was sounded; drums rolled; guards came running; the prisoners were bundled away to quarters. Sir Sydney, from his room, caught sight of the watcher opposite and made frantic signals. They were understood. By the time the head jailer and the officers he summoned had traced the matter to the right house, and discovered the tunnel—no one was there.

"I feared as much," muttered the valet John, when the two friends could exchange a word later. "They got away all right, but they failed. They'll always fail."

"What? You, of all persons, have lost heart?" exclaimed Smith. The other nodded despondently, glanced at his fantastic garments, and spat out a curse.

"Yes; I give up. If all the efforts made to free the royal family from these very rooms could not succeed, how can we succeed? I'm about ready to give up, tell them my name, and let them kill me."

"Don't be a fool! I'll tell you how we can succeed!" exclaimed Smith with a burst of passionate energy. Then he caught sight of a flicker at the doorwicket. His tone changed instantly. "You lazy, disgraceful rascal, look at these boots of mine! You were supposed to have cleaned them. You've nothing else to do, and yet you neglect your work like a damned surly dog!"

He buffeted the Marquis in furious anger. There was a low laugh outside the door; the guard, satisfied, withdrew. Taifort rubbed his cheek and grinned.

"Well done; they nearly caught us. Well, how to succeed, then?"

"The simplest way, of course—always the simplest way!" exclaimed Sir Sydney. "I never thought of it before; of course, of course! All this slow, laborious effort is sheer waste of time."

"I agree with you. What, then, is your way of simplicity?"

Sir Sydney made a gesture of caution.

"Tell you later—when I think it out."

This attempted rescue of the prisoners kicked up a fearful row. That Smith was the objective, could be guessed; he was the most important prisoner in French hands, and the most closely guarded.

His little promenades were brought to light. The Directory, who ruled France, did not know whether to be lost in admiration of his quixotic sense of honor, or in fury at the chief jailer's trust in him. Lasne was removed at once, and another took his place.

John's wife did not reappear. The bribed guard, no doubt in fear lest his bribery become known, refused with vicious oaths even to speak with Sir Sydney. All communication with the outside was cut off—but not before Smith had smuggled out a note directed to his friends in England.

The result of this became apparent one morning, when the valet John was summoned to pack his effects and clear out. As a prisoner of war, he had been exchanged.

Hearing this, he gazed at Sir Sydney with actual dismay.

"But I can't leave you alone here! How this was managed, I don't know—"

"I do," said Smith, laughing. "I arranged it, my friend. You're in more danger than I am. I simply directed England to effect your exchange at once—the simplest way, you understand? It should have been done months ago, a year ago! Unfortunately, I had not learned my lesson then. Now I have. You shall go, and become the means of rescuing me."

"I?" demanded the other. "How?"

Smith, who appeared to be in excellent spirits, whispered in his ear, and drew back, laughing at the astonishment of the other.

"The simplest way—you see?" he observed. "You can get word to agents here in Paris; the whole thing is a matter of half an hour."

"You're out of your head!" ejaculated the valet John, staring at him. "But I'll tell them. Good-by, my dear kind master," he added, as guards appeared. "It grieves me to part with you—"

"It doesn't grieve me," broke in Smith. "You're an idle, lazy rogue, and I'm glad to be rid of you!"

Thus the Marquis de Taifort, ridiculous jockey rig and all, departed from the scene, safely reaching England with a batch of exchanged prisoners.

T H E   R I G O R of Sir Sydney Smith's confinement was redoubled by the new jailer. He received no favors, no liberty; new and more severe orders were received from the Directory, and were obeyed harshly.

"If the accursed English hope to get you out of here," said the jailer, after changing him from the moderately comfortable rooms to close solitary confinement, "they'll have to conquer all Paris!"

"Ultimately," said Sir Sydney, with his gay smile, "they'll probably do just that, my friend!"

Upon a late Saturday afternoon, word was brought to the prison governor of a carriage at the gates, containing Adjutant L'Oger and Colonel Lafarge, on official business. He ordered the carriage admitted, and received the two officers with ceremony.

"Citizen," said the adjutant, throwing down a document, "the

"So!" Sir Sydney exclaimed indignantly. "I'm
to receive still further persecutions?"

Directory desires to transfer one of your guests to less comfortable but perhaps safer quarters. Here's the order. If you'll be so
good as to hand him over to us, we'll be on our way."

"Eh? The Englishman?" The jailer seized the document,

examined the signatures of Barras and other directors, the seal, the stamp of the minister. "A moment, citizens, till the registrar assures me that all is correct."

He bustled away to the *greffier* or registrar, who presently returned with him and sent for the prisoner. Sir Sydney was brought in between two guards, and informed that he was to change prisons.

"So!" he exclaimed indignantly. "I'm to receive still further persecutions? As though I were not bad enough off here—"

"Citizen," broke in the adjutant stiffly, "the Government does not wish to aggravate your misfortunes. You'll be very comfortable in the place to which I'm taking you." And as he spoke, Adjutant L'Oger winked significantly at the prison governor, who grinned in delight at the jest, and then motioned the guards.

"Take him away, help pack his effects, and be smart about it."

As the officials waited, the governor and chief jailer beckoned the registrar.

"Give the Citizen Adjutant the book; the discharge must be signed."

The big book was produced; the discharge was written in; and Adjutant L'Oger signed it with a flourish.

"You have no guards?" asked the registrar anxiously.

"I," said Colonel Lafarge promptly, "am in charge of the prisoner."

At this moment Sir Sydney was brought back, with his personal belongings. The registrar nodded.

"Yes, Citizen Colonel, but you must take at least six of our men properly to guard this man. He is most important."

"Nonsense!" exclaimed Lafarge, and turned to Smith. "I am an officer; you're an officer. Your parole will be sufficient to do away with an escort. Your honor is well known."

Smith bowed. "Thank you. I swear on the faith of an officer to accompany you wherever you may take me."

"Enough! To the carriage," said Adjutant L'Oger, and out they went.

The carriage rolled away. The gates clanged shut. On the strength of a forged order, Sir Sydney Smith was out of prison and on his way to freedom—a matter of half an hour's work in all.

"SO," CONCLUDED Cotterel, smiling, "you see the lesson, my friend? Circumstances alter cases, in other words. When all else is useless, the simplest way may succeed."

Old Manning wakened from his absorbed attention, came back to the present, and with a sigh glanced around the infirmary.

"That may be true," he said, on his nimble fingers: "but I don't see why it should apply to my case. Unless,"—and he suddenly transfixed Cotterel with a startled, intent look,—"unless you have some crazy scheme!"

The younger man, indeed, was suddenly in obvious suspense. He glanced at his watch, frowned, and wiped beads of perspiration from his forehead.

"Yes," he admitted. "Yes, I—I had a scheme—but I don't know—"

"Good Lord, man!" The other stared at him, aghast. "What have you done? You haven't forged anything—"

Cotterel made an urgent signal of caution, as the door opened and the prison doctor came in. He went to Manning seized his hand, and pumped it, beaming at him.

"Upon my word, Manning, I'm delighted! I understand there's some good news for you. Anyway, you're wanted in the Warden's office. You can walk, all right; shall I have an orderly help you dress?"

"No, no, I'll do it," broke in Cotterel anxiously. "We'll be ready in five minutes, Doc."

"I'll be waiting." And the other departed.

Alone, Manning caught Cotterel by the arms, stared into his face, then freed his hands to talk.

"Answer me! Don't you know that forged papers will only make more trouble later? What in the devil's name have you done?"

"Taken Sir Sydney's advice," said Cotterel with a shaky laugh. "I went about it the simplest way, that's all. You know, the Governor was much interested in my case, on account of my proven innocence. It wasn't hard to see him. I got him interested in you. He almost agreed to parole you in my care, to Arizona. Said he'd get in touch with the Warden this afternoon, by telephone. This means that he's decided. He's done it. You're going with me—away, free—understand?"

Manning turned away, to hide the tears on his cheeks.

"But why," he asked, when he was dressed and ready, "why didn't you tell me before?"

"I wasn't sure," said Cotterel in wild delight. "Don't you see? I didn't dare give you hope that would only be dashed. I tried to break it to you with that story while I sparred for time, and waited for the word to come through. Old man, you're walking out now—thank Heaven, we're done with all this forever!"

And they were.

ABOUT THE AUTHOR

H. BEDFORD-JONES is a Canadian by birth, but not by profession, having removed to the United States at the age of one year. For over twenty years he has been more or less profitably engaged in writing and traveling. As he has seldom resided in one place longer than a year or so and is a person of retiring habits, he is somewhat a man of mystery; more than once he has suffered from unscrupulous gentlemen who impersonated him—one of whom murdered a wife and was subsequently shot by the police, luckily after losing his alias.

The real Bedford-Jones is an elderly man, whose gray hair and precise attire give him rather the appearance of a retired foreign diplomat. His hobby is stamp collecting, and his collection of Japan is said to be one of the finest in existence. At present writing he is en route to Morocco, and when this appears in print he will probably be somewhere on the Mojave Desert in company with Erle Stanley Gardner.

Questioned as to the main facts in his life, he declared there was only one main fact, but it was not for publication; that his life had been uneventful except for numerous financial losses, and that his only adventures lay in evading adventurers. In his younger years he was something of an athlete, but the encroachments of age preclude any active pursuits except that of motoring. He is usually to be found poring over his stamps, working at his typewriter, or laboring in his California rose garden, which is one of the sights of Cathedral Cañon, near Palm Springs.

www.ingramcontent.com/pod-product-compliance
Lightning Source LLC
Chambersburg PA
CBHW061524020726

47502CB00006B/2222